Chloe

A CHRISTMAS NOVEL

ANGEL INSTITUTE
BOOK FOUR

ERICA PENROD

Dear Reader,

We're so delighted you're here! Welcome to Angel Institute, where romance, Christmas magic, and angels-in-training come together to share the Spirit of Christmas right in the heart of Benton Falls.

This series draws inspiration from some of the most beloved Christmas classics, including—but certainly not limited to—*It's a Wonderful Life*, *A Christmas Carol*, *White Christmas*, and, of course, the greatest story ever told—the birth of our Savior, Jesus Christ, when angels proclaimed tidings of great joy.

As you journey through these stories, we hope you'll feel the wonder of the season, the warmth of love for your family and sweetheart, and, most importantly, the deep love God has for you.

Heaven is always mindful of you, dear friend. There are angels all around you, cheering you on and working for your good. Our prayer is that as you read, you'll recognize their presence, feel their support, and rejoice with them this Christmas.

Merry Christmas!

Lucy & Erica

Prologue

REBECCA

T he celestial chimes ring out, their annoyingly perfect tones cutting through my last-minute scroll through HaloHub—heaven's social media. I roll my eyes, reluctantly pocketing my phone and smoothing down my shimmering robe. It's like wearing a prom dress 24/7, I swear. As I plop down into my seat at the Angel Institute's classroom, the wooden chair lets out a pathetic creak. Great, even the furniture here is goody-two-shoes, apologizing for making noise.

I glance around the room, trying not to look too impressed. The walls are doing their usual dance of golden light, like some cosmic lava lamp. Above us, the ceiling's gone into full planetarium mode, stars twinkling away like they're auditioning for a celestial talent show. It's beautiful, sure, but would it kill them to change it up once in a while? Maybe some clouds, or I don't know, a supernova?

My fingers drum an impatient rhythm on the desk.

It's cool and smooth, probably some heavenly wood that never gets splinters. Glowing symbols pulse beneath my fingertips, and I trace one absentmindedly. A little zap of divine energy shoots through me, and I jerk my hand back. Seriously? Even the furniture's trying to teach us lessons now?

The air's thick with the smell of celestial flowers—jasmine mixed with something so pure it makes my nose itch. It's like being stuck in a heavenly Bath & Body Works. I miss the smell of coffee, of city streets after rain, of anything real and a little bit messy.

As I wait for our mentor to arrive, I can't help but feel a twinge of frustration. This isn't where I expected to be at 22. In my earthly life, I was Rebecca Goldstein, a driven and successful young woman with big dreams and even bigger ambitions—until I had run in with a bus and the bus won.

But here I am, stuck in guardian angel training—the only way out of my current heavenly vocation. My perfectly manicured nails tap an impatient rhythm on the desk as I recall my initial excitement at being assigned the role of heavenly weather forecaster. I thought it would be prestigious, important. Instead, it's become a source of mockery among the other angels. After all, what's the point of predicting weather in a realm of perpetual sunshine and warmth—there are only so many ways to say, "sunny and clear".

The sound of approaching footsteps pulls me from my brooding. Henry, our mentor, enters the room with his usual air of genial authority. His silver hair catches the starlight, creating a halo effect that reminds me of the illustrations in children's Bible stories. His kind blue eyes twinkle as he surveys the class, and I feel a mixture of affection and exasperation. Henry's unfailing optimism is both endearing and grating to my more cynical nature.

"Good morning, my dear angels in training," Henry greets us, his voice warm and rich like honey. "I trust you're all ready for another day of learning and growth?"

A chorus of enthusiastic responses fills the air. I mumble a half-hearted "Yes, Henry," trying to muster some semblance of excitement. Henry's gaze lingers on me for a moment, and I see a flicker of understanding in his eyes. He knows I'm struggling, but he never pushes or criticizes. It's the thing I grudgingly admire about him.

"Today, we're going to discuss a very special aspect of our duties as guardian angels," Henry begins, moving to stand behind the intricately carved wooden lectern at the front of the room. "We'll be exploring the concept of divine intervention and how we can guide our charges towards their true paths without infringing upon their free will."

I lean forward slightly, my interest piqued despite myself. This sounds more substantial than our usual lessons on angel etiquette—like not popping in on them in the restroom.

"Remember," Henry continues, his voice taking on a more serious tone, "our role is not to make decisions for the humans in our care, but to gently nudge them towards the light. We are guides, not puppeteers."

As Henry speaks, I feel a familiar sense of restlessness

stirring within me. I want to do more, to make a real difference. Predicting sunny days and balmy breezes seems so... inconsequential.

"Rebecca," Henry's voice cuts through my thoughts, startling me. "Would you care to share your thoughts on the balance between guidance and free will?"

I blink, surprised. "Well," I begin, trying to gather my thoughts, "I suppose it's about... providing opportunities? Showing them the right path without forcing them down it?"

Henry nods encouragingly. "That's a good start. Can you elaborate on how you might apply this in your current role?"

I feel a flush of embarrassment creep up my neck. "In my weather forecasting?" I ask, unable to keep the note of disdain from my voice. "I'm not sure how predicting perfect weather day after day really guides anyone, Henry."

A ripple of whispers and giggles passes through the classroom. I lift my chin defiantly, expecting a reprimand. But Henry just smiles, his eyes twinkling with that infuriating, knowing look.

"Ah, Rebecca," he says gently. "You're so focused on the grandeur of the task that you're missing its true significance. Tell me, how do you think your forecasts affect the moods of those around you?"

I pause, considering. "I... I suppose a sunny forecast might make them happier?" I venture hesitantly.

Henry beams. "Exactly. And how might that happiness influence their actions, their interactions with others?"

As the implications of his words sink in, I feel a slight shift in my perspective. Could my seemingly trivial job actually have a ripple effect on the entire heavenly community?

"I see you're beginning to understand," Henry says softly. "Every role, no matter how small it may seem, has the potential to create significant change. It's not about the task itself, but the spirit with which we approach it."

I nod slowly, a mixture of emotions swirling within me. Part of me still longs for something more dramatic, more obviously important. But I can't deny the logic in Henry's words.

"Now," Henry continues, addressing the entire class once more, "I have some exciting news. It's time for your final assignments."

A buzz of excitement fills the room. My heart races. This is it—a chance to prove myself, to do something more than recite the weather.

Henry begins calling out names and handing out scrolls. I listen with growing impatience, waiting to hear mine. Finally, Henry turns to me.

"Rebecca," he says, his voice warm but serious. "Your assignment." He hands me a scroll of ivory parchment with a gold seal.

"Thanks." I accept the paper and feel a surge of excitement mixed with a touch of apprehension. Unrolling the scroll, I take a deep breath and read:

Dear Celestial Trainee,

Your final examination has arrived. This Christmas season, you are tasked with a mission of utmost importance—one that will determine your readiness to receive your wings and ascend to the honored rank of guardian angel.

You are hereby assigned to assist:

Chloe Anderson a successful business owner

Your objective is to help this individual discover and embrace the true spirit of giving this Christmas.

Your success hinges on Chloe's genuine understanding and application of this essential Christmas virtue.

Be advised: the stakes are high. A successful mission will earn you your wings and the privilege of becoming a guardian angel. However, failure to complete this task satisfactorily will result in a century-long delay before you may attempt this final test again.

May the light of Heaven guide you in this crucial endeavor. We have the utmost faith in your abilities.

Wishing you divine success,

The Angelic High Council

Hmph, I scrunch my nose as I look at Arthur, my fellow angel in training. "The spirit of giving. At least I might not have to use the words 'sunny and bright' for a week or two." Ruben grins and I read the letter once more, not sure what I expected.

This sounds like a real challenge—exactly what I've been craving. But as I think about the task ahead, I realize how unprepared I feel. How am I supposed to guide someone back to the spirit of giving when I'm still grappling with my own sense of purpose?

"Remember," Henry says, as if reading my thoughts, "this assignment isn't just about helping Chloe. It's also an opportunity for your own growth. To truly guide someone towards the light, we must first find it within ourselves."

I nod, trying to project confidence even as doubts swirl in my mind. Can I really do this? Am I capable of earning my wings?

As the class disperses, buzzing with excitement about their assignments, Henry waits at the door, congratulating and encouraging his students. I approach the door as Henry places a gentle hand on my shoulder, and I feel a warm surge of comfort and strength flow through me.

"Rebecca," he says softly, "I know you've been struggling with your role here. But I want you to know that I see great potential in you. This assignment... it's not just about Chloe. It's about you, too. About helping you understand the true meaning of service, of using your gifts to bring light to others."

I look up at him, surprised by the depth of emotion

in his eyes. "But Henry," I protest weakly, "You know who I am...or who I was, right? Service was never my thing. I'm not sure I can guide someone else?"

Henry's smile is gentle but firm. "Sometimes, my dear, the best way to learn is by teaching. Trust in the process. Trust in yourself. And most importantly, trust in the divine plan that has brought you to this moment."

As Henry's words sink in, I feel a subtle shift within me. The frustration and restlessness that have been my constant companions take a step back, giving me enough space to move in a different direction.

I stand, smoothing down my robe once more. "Thank you, Henry," I say, my voice stronger now. "I... I'll do my best."

"That's all anyone can ask," Henry replies with a warm smile. "Now, off you go. Your journey begins now."

As I leave the classroom and step into the hallway, I catch a glimpse of myself in the shimmering wall. My long, golden hair seems to glow with an inner light, and my eyes—usually a clear blue—have taken on a soft, violet hue that reminds me of the twilight sky. I straighten my shoulders, trying to project the confidence I don't quite feel yet.

I may not have wings, I may not be able to fly or wield heavenly weapons, but I am a guardian angel in training. I have a mission to complete and I don't like to fail.

With a deep breath, I make my way through the celestial halls, preparing for my descent to Earth. I can't help but wonder what awaits me. Will I be able to help Chloe rediscover the spirit of giving and, therefore, Christmas? And in doing so, will I finally understand my place in this divine plan?

I hope so.

I'd like to feel like I belonged here. Ever since I got here—going on 5 years now—I've wondered why my earthly life was cut short, why I didn't get to live out my dreams, and for what? To be a weather forecaster, where nothing is required of me, but to repeat one sentence over and over again?

And now I've got my chance. To show Henry and everyone else on the council that I deserve my wings, that I'm deserving of the honor.

I straighten my back and smooth my hair, tucking the scroll inside the pocket of my robe. I'm ready.

With one last look at the shimmering, star-filled skies of heaven, I close my eyes and prepare for my journey. Whatever happens, I know this experience will change me forever. And as I feel the pull towards Earth beginning to envelop me, I whisper a quiet prayer, because even I know I can't do this without the help.

"Guide me, give me strength, and help me be the angel Chloe needs."

I close my eyes and journey from the heavenly realm, ready to begin my mission on Earth. The adventure has only just begun.

One

CHLOE

The sharp staccato of my heels echoes through the sleek hallways of Anderson Tech as I stride towards my office. The scent of freshly brewed coffee drifts from the break room, mingling with the clean smell of new electronics. It's a familiar aroma, one that usually energizes me, but today it does little to lift my mood.

I push open the glass door to my office, the cool surface smooth beneath my palm. The expansive room greets me with its minimalist décor—all chrome, glass, and stark white surfaces. It's a testament to my success, a far cry from the cramped, dingy apartment of my childhood. Yet today, it feels hollow somehow.

Settling into my ergonomic chair, I boot up my computer and pull up the latest metrics for our newest app. The numbers are impressive—downloads skyrocketing, user engagement off the charts. I should feel elated, triumphant even. Instead, I feel... nothing.

A gentle knock at the door interrupts my thoughts. "Come in," I call out, not bothering to look up from my screen.

"Ms. Anderson?" My assistant, Sally, pokes her head in. "The board is waiting for you in the conference room."

I nod curtly, rising from my chair. "Thank you, Sally. I'll be right there."

As I make my way to the conference room, I catch a glimpse of my reflection in the floor-to-ceiling windows. My dark hair is impeccably styled, my tailored suit crisp and wrinkle-free. I look every inch the successful CEO. But my blue eyes, usually sharp and focused, seem distant today.

The conference room falls silent as I enter. Ten pairs of eyes turn to me, a mixture of respect and expectation in their gazes. I take my seat at the head of the table, the leather chair cool against my back.

"Good morning, everyone," I begin, my voice steady and confident. "Let's get started, shall we?"

For the next hour, I lead the meeting with practiced ease. We discuss quarterly projections, marketing strategies, and potential expansions. The board members nod approvingly as I present our latest successes. On the surface, everything is perfect.

As the meeting wraps up, Harold, one of the older board members, clears his throat. "Before we adjourn, there's one more matter to discuss." He pauses, his kind eyes meeting mine. "Chloe, we've noticed you've been working non-stop for months now, actually years. We cannot even think of a time in the past four years that you have taken a vacation, not even holidays. You worked through Thanksgiving just last week. With Christmas coming up, we think it's time you took a break."

I feel my body tense, my fingers gripping the armrests of my chair. "That's not necessary," I say, forcing a smile. "I'm perfectly capable of managing my own time."

Harold shakes his head gently. "It's not a suggestion, Chloe. It's a decision we've all agreed on. You need to take some time off. At least until after Christmas."

The words hit me like a physical blow. Christmas. The very thought of it makes my stomach churn. Memories of cold, lonely holidays spent in foster homes flash through my mind. The pitying looks, the secondhand gifts, the constant reminder that I didn't belong.

"I appreciate your concern," I say, my voice tight, "but I assure you, I don't need a break. Especially not during the holidays."

"Chloe," Harold's voice is gentle but firm, "you've done an incredible job building this company. But even the most successful CEOs need time to recharge. We're not asking you to take a vacation. Just... go home. Spend some time away from the office. Enjoy the season."

I want to argue, to insist that I'm fine, that the company needs me. But I can see the determination in their eyes. This isn't a battle I'm going to win.

"Fine," I concede, my tone clipped. "I'll take some time off. But I'll be checking in regularly, and if anything urgent comes up—"

"We'll handle it," Harold assures me. "You've built a

strong team here, Chloe. Trust them to keep things running smoothly for a few weeks."

With that, the meeting adjourns. As the board members file out, offering well-wishes for my forced vacation, I remain seated, staring out the window at the city skyline. The early December sun glints off the skyscrapers, and in the distance, I can see workers setting up an enormous Christmas tree in the city square.

My mind drifts to the small town of Benton Falls, where my grandmother's house sits empty. It's been years since I've visited, not since her funeral. The thought of spending Christmas there, alone in that old house, should be depressing. Instead, I feel a sense of relief. At least there, I won't have to pretend to enjoy the forced cheer of the season.

Back in my office, I start making arrangements. I cancel my social engagements—not that there were many to begin with—and book a flight to the small regional airport near Benton Falls. As I pack up my laptop, Sally appears in the doorway.

"Ms. Anderson? I've just received an invitation for you," she says hesitantly. "The mayor of Benton Falls is inviting you to attend their annual Tree Lighting Ceremony. It's tomorrow night."

How in the world would anyone know I was coming to Benton Falls? I'd only decided on the trip two hours ago. I suppress a sigh. Of course, word of my impending arrival has already spread. Small towns and their gossip. "Thank you, Sally. Please send my regrets. I won't be attending any events during my stay."

Sally nods, but I catch a flicker of disappointment in her eyes. "Of course, Ms. Anderson. Is there anything else you need before you leave?"

For a moment, I'm tempted to ask her to cancel everything, to tell the board I've changed my mind. Instead, I shake my head. "No, that will be all. Thank you, Sally. I'll see you after the New Year."

As Sally leaves, I sink back into my chair, suddenly feeling exhausted. The thought of weeks alone in Benton Falls stretches before me, a mix of dread and strange anticipation churning in my stomach.

I close my eyes, memories of my childhood flooding back unbidden. The constant moves from one foster home to another, after my grandmother passed away. She was supposed to rescue me, to help me after my parents passed, but then she was taken too. I was left all alone in the world. I remember the pain and the loneliness. The struggle to fit in, to prove my worth. The realization that in this world, money equals security, respect, power. I've worked so hard to leave that scared, lonely little girl behind. To become someone strong, successful, untouchable.

But as I sit here in my plush office, surrounded by the trappings of my success, I can't shake the feeling that something's missing. That despite all I've achieved, there's a hollow space inside me that no amount of money or accolades can fill.

With a sigh, I push these thoughts aside. There's no use dwelling on the past or on vague feelings of discontent. I have a company to run, even if it's from a distance.

Opening my eyes, I compose an email to my team, outlining my expectations for their performance in my absence.

The next morning, I find myself on a small commuter plane, watching the sprawling city give way to rolling hills and dense forests. As we descend towards the regional airport, I catch my first glimpse of Benton Falls in years. From above, it looks like something out of a Christmas card—quaint buildings with snow-dusted roofs, winding streets lined with trees, a picturesque town square dominated by an imposing courthouse.

A wave of nostalgia washes over me, memories of childhood summers spent here with my grandmother. For a moment, I allow myself to remember the warmth of her hugs, the smell of her homemade apple pie, the sound of her laughter. But I quickly push these thoughts away. That was a different time, a different me. I'm here to work in peace, not to indulge in sentimental reminiscence.

As the plane touches down with a gentle bump, I steel myself for what's to come. Four weeks in Benton Falls. I can do this. I'll keep my head down, focus on work, and before I know it, I'll be back in the city where I belong.

The drive from the airport to my grandmother's house is a journey through a winter wonderland. Snow blankets the fields on either side of the road, and bare trees glisten with icicles. Despite myself, I feel a small spark of childlike wonder at the beauty of it all.

As I turn onto Maple Street, where my grandmother's house sits, I'm struck by how little has changed. The same old Victorian homes line the street, their gingerbread trim and wrap-around porches looking like something out of a Norman Rockwell painting. Christmas decorations adorn every porch and yard - twinkling lights, cheerful inflatable Santas, carefully arranged nativity scenes.

And then I see it—my grandmother's house. Or rather, my house now. The small craftsman bungalow sits back from the street, its yellow paint warm and inviting against the snowy backdrop. But as I pull into the driveway, I feel my jaw drop in disbelief.

The house is decorated for Christmas. Twinkling white lights outline the roof and porch. A classic wreath with red berries and an enormous bow hangs on the deep green front door. Through the ornate front window, I can see the soft glow of what must be a Christmas tree.

For a moment, I sit in the car, stunned. Who could have done this? How did they get into the house? A mix of anger and confusion swirls in my chest as I grab my bags and march up to the front door.

The key turns smoothly in the lock, and as I step inside, I'm enveloped by the scent of pine and cinnamon. The interior of the house is just as festive as the outside. Evergreen garlands and holly adorn the walls, stockings hang from the fireplace mantel, and sure enough, a small Christmas tree stands in the corner of the living room, its lights twinkling softly.

I drop my bags, my mind racing. This has to be some kind of mistake. Maybe the cleaning company thought they were doing me a favor, preparing the house for my arrival. But as I move further into the house, taking in the vintage-style sage green cabinetry in the kitchen, the soft quilts draped over the furniture, I realize that this goes beyond simple decoration. The house looks lived in, loved.

Just as I'm about to call the local police station to report a possible break-in, there's a knock at the door. My heart races as I approach it cautiously. Who could it be? The mysterious decorator? A nosy neighbor?

Taking a deep breath, I open the door. Standing on my porch is a young woman about my age, her long golden hair catching the late afternoon sunlight. Her bright eyes—are they blue? Green? I can't quite tell—twinkle with a mixture of friendliness and something else I can't quite place.

"Hi there," she says brightly. "I'm Rebecca. I live next door. I saw you pull up and thought I'd come over to welcome you to the neighborhood."

I blink, taken aback by her cheerful demeanor. "I'm Chloe," I reply automatically, then hesitate. Should I ask her about the decorations? Demand to know what's going on?

Before I can decide, Rebecca continues, "I hope you don't mind, but when we heard Marge's granddaughter was coming to stay for Christmas, we couldn't resist sprucing the place up a bit. It's a bit of a tradition here in Benton Falls—no one spends the holidays in an undecorated home."

Her words hit me like a physical blow. The entire

neighborhood knew I was coming? They took it upon themselves to decorate my house? A mix of emotions swirls within me—anger at the invasion of privacy, confusion at their presumption, and underneath it all, a tiny flicker of something that feels dangerously like gratitude.

"That's... very thoughtful," I manage to say, my voice stiffer than I intend. "But it really wasn't necessary. I'm only here for a short while, and I'm not particularly interested in celebrating the holidays."

Rebecca's smile falters for just a moment before brightening again. "Well, decorated or not, we're glad to have you here. Will you be attending the Tree Lighting Ceremony tonight? It's quite the event—the whole town turns out for it."

I shake my head firmly. "No, I'm afraid I'll have to miss it. I have a lot of work to catch up on."

A little lie, but I'm not expecting Santa to bring me presents, anyway.

"Oh." Rebecca's disappointment is palpable, but she rallies quickly. "Well, if you change your mind, it starts at 7 PM in the town square. You can't miss it—just follow the crowds and the smell of hot chocolate."

I nod noncommittally, already planning my escape from this overly friendly interaction. "Thank you for stopping by, Rebecca. I should really get unpacked now."

"Of course." Rebecca steps back, still smiling. "Don't be a stranger, Chloe. And welcome to Benton Falls."

As I close the door, I lean against it, suddenly feeling exhausted. This is exactly what I was afraid of—the forced cheer, the expectations, the assumption that everyone must love Christmas. I glance around at the festive decorations, feeling more out of place than ever.

With a sigh, I pick up my bags and head to the bedroom. To my relief, it seems to have escaped the worst of the holiday makeover. I unpack quickly, hanging my clothes in the vintage wardrobe that still smells faintly of cedar and my grandmother's perfume.

As night falls, I settle on the couch with my laptop, determined to lose myself in work. But the twinkling lights of the Christmas tree keep catching my eye, and the scent of the holiday seems to permeate everything. Despite my best efforts, memories of past Christmases creep in.

I remember my first Christmas after my grandmother died, spent in a group home. The sad little tree with its sparse decorations, the meager gifts that were more necessity than joy. I remember promising myself then that I would never be in that position again. That I would work hard, become successful, ensure that I never had to rely on anyone's charity or pity.

And I've done it. I've built a life for myself beyond my wildest childhood dreams. So why does sitting here in this cozy, Christmas-filled house make me feel so... empty?

I shake my head, banishing these thoughts. I'm here to work, not to dwell on the past or get swept up in a small-town Christmas cheer. Opening my email, I immerse myself in reports and projections, letting the familiar world of numbers and strategies wash away the uncomfortable emotions.

As midnight approaches, I finally close my laptop. The house is quiet, the only sound the soft ticking of the old grandfather clock in the hall. I make my way to the bedroom, studiously avoiding looking at the Christmas decorations.

Lying in bed, staring up at the unfamiliar ceiling, I can't shake the feeling that coming here was a mistake. I don't belong in this world of neighborly kindness and Christmas traditions. I've worked too hard to build my walls, to protect myself from the pain and disappointment that comes with letting people in.

Tomorrow, I decide, I'll call the office. Surely there's some crisis that requires my immediate attention, some reason for me to cut this enforced vacation short. I'll go back to Boston, back to the world I understand, where success is measured in dollars and cents, not in twinkling lights and warm smiles.

As I drift off to sleep, I try to ignore the small voice in the back of my mind, the one that whispers that maybe, just maybe, I'm running away from something more than just Christmas cheer. That perhaps what I'm really afraid of is not the possibility of failure, but the terrifying prospect of letting myself feel again, of opening my heart to the warmth and joy that seems to permeate this little town.

But those are dangerous thoughts, ones that threaten the carefully constructed world I've built for myself. So I push them away, burying them deep beneath layers of determination and ambition. I'm successful CEO and have built a billion-dollar company. I don't need Christmas, and I certainly don't need the pity or charity of a small town stuck in the past.

As sleep finally claims me, my last conscious thought is a determination to remain aloof, to resist the pull of Benton Falls and its Christmas magic. Little do I know that the universe—and a certain guardian angel in training - have other plans for me this holiday season.

Two

CHLOE

The morning sun assaults my eyes as I wake, momentarily disoriented by the unfamiliar surroundings. The scent of pine lingers in the air, a constant reminder of the unwanted holiday cheer that has invaded this space.

With a groan, I reach for my phone, eager to dive back into the familiar world of emails and business reports. But as I scroll through my inbox, my frown deepens. No urgent messages. No crises to manage. Just a smattering of routine updates and well-wishes for my "vacation."

Frustration bubbles up inside me. Don't they understand I don't do vacations? That every moment away from the office is a moment wasted?

I toss aside the covers and pad to the window, peering out at the snow-covered street below. Benton Falls is already awake, its residents bustling about their day. I watch as a group of children trudge by, their laughter floating up to me as they pelt each other with snowballs.

For a fleeting moment, I feel a pang of... something. Longing? Regret? I quickly push it aside. I made my choices long ago. This quaint, small-town life isn't for me. It never was.

But as the morning wears on, cabin fever sets in. The walls of the house seem to close in around me, the cheerful decorations mocking my attempts to focus on work. By mid-afternoon, I can't take it anymore. I need to get out, to remind myself that there's a world beyond this Christmas-obsessed town.

Bundling up in my designer coat and boots, I step out into the brisk winter air. The cold bites at my cheeks, but it's refreshing after the stuffy warmth of the house. I make my way towards the town square, my heels clicking against the shoveled sidewalk.

As I round the corner, the full splendor of Benton Falls during Christmas comes into view. The town square is a winter wonderland, with twinkling lights adorning every tree and lamppost. A massive Christmas tree stands proudly in the center, its ornaments glinting in the afternoon sun. The air is filled with the sounds of carols drifting from hidden speakers and the chatter of townspeople going about their holiday shopping.

Despite myself, I feel a flicker of appreciation for the scene. It's like something out of a Hallmark movie— picturesque, idyllic, and completely divorced from reality.

As I wander the square, my gaze is drawn to a storefront I remember from my childhood visits. Hanks' Department Store stands as a testament to a bygone era, its large frosted windows showcasing elaborate holiday displays. Vintage toys, twinkling lights, and festive garlands create miniature winter scenes that have a small crowd of children pressed against the glass, their eyes wide with wonder.

A memory surfaces, unbidden. Me, at seven years old, nose pressed against that very window, longing for a beautiful doll I knew we could never afford. The ache of want, the burning shame of poverty...

I shake my head, banishing the thought. That was a lifetime ago. I'm not that little girl anymore.

Squaring my shoulders, I march towards the store and feel a sense of relief as the business part of my brain has kicked in, seeing potential where others might only see nostalgia. If I could convince this store to use my app, to modernize their operations, it could be the perfect case study for expanding into small-town markets.

The bell above the door jingles merrily as I step inside, and I'm immediately enveloped in a cocoon of warmth and the scent of cinnamon and cloves. The interior of the store is even more of a throwback than the outside, with high ceilings adorned with ornate moldings and brass chandeliers casting a warm glow over the merchandise.

Wooden display tables are laden with carefully arranged holiday gifts, everything from plush toys to fine scarves, all wrapped in bright, festive paper. A grand staircase, its banister wrapped in evergreen garlands and twinkling lights, leads to a second floor that promises even more wares.

It's charming, in an outdated sort of way. But all I can see are the inefficiencies, the missed opportunities for streamlining and modernization.

"Need a hand with anything?"

The deep, gravelly voice startles me out of my mental inventory. I turn to find myself face to face with a man who could have stepped right out of a lumberjack calendar. Tall and broad-shouldered, with tousled sandy brown hair and piercing hazel eyes, he exudes an aura of rugged charm, even though he's dressed in a sky blue dress shirt and matching tie. His smile is genuine but reserved, a stark contrast to the polished, practiced grins I'm used to in the corporate world.

"Name's Oliver Hanks," he continues, extending a calloused hand. "Welcome to my store."

I take his hand, noting the strength of his grip and the slight roughness of his palm. This is a man who's no stranger to hard work.

"Chloe Anderson," I reply, slipping easily into my professional persona. "I was just admiring your... unique setup here."

Oliver's smile widens slightly. "Well, we aim to be one-of-a-kind. Looking for anything special? Gift for someone?"

I shake my head. "Actually, Mr. Hanks, I'm here on business. I'm the CEO of Anderson Tech, and I couldn't help but notice the potential for modernization in your store."

Oliver's smile falters, his brow furrowing. "Modernization? What are you getting at, Ms. Anderson?"

I launch into my pitch; the words flowing easily after countless investor meetings and product launches. "Your store has charm, Mr. Hanks, but it's falling behind the times. With my company's app, you could streamline your inventory management, implement a modern point-of-sale system, even set up an online storefront. We could bring Hanks' Department Store into the 21st century."

As I speak, I can see Oliver's expression shifting from confusion to something that looks unsettlingly like amusement. When I finish, he lets out a short, gruff laugh that sets my teeth on edge.

"Look, Ms. Anderson," he says, his tone firm and unyielding. "I appreciate the offer, but Hanks' isn't just a business. It's part of Benton Falls. Our customers don't come here for efficiency or some fancy app. They come for the experience, for the personal touch you can't get from a screen."

I feel a flare of irritation. Why can't he see the opportunity I'm offering? "Mr. Hanks, I understand the value of tradition, but you can't ignore progress. In today's market-"

"In today's market," Oliver interrupts, his voice low and intense, "people are starved for connection. That's what we offer here. Not just products, but a place where folks can meet, where kids can experience Christmas shopping like their parents and grandparents did."

I open my mouth to argue further, but Oliver holds

up a hand. "I get it. You're trying to help. But Hanks' isn't interested in being a guinea pig for your tech company. Now, if you want to do some actual shopping, I'd be happy to point you in the right direction."

The dismissal in his words is clear, and I feel my cheeks burn with a mixture of embarrassment and anger. How dare he dismiss me so easily? Doesn't he know who I am?

But before I can formulate a suitably cutting response, the bell above the door chimes again. A group of elderly women enter, calling out greetings to Oliver by name. In an instant, his attention is diverted, his face softening as he welcomes the newcomers.

I stand there for a moment, feeling strangely out of place in my designer outfit amidst the homey charm of the store. Oliver's words echo in my mind, challenging everything I've built my life and career around.

With a huff of frustration, I turn on my heel and march out of the store, the cheerful jingle of the bell seeming to mock me as I go. The cold air hits me like a slap as I step outside, and I welcome it, using the sting to push away the unsettling feelings Oliver's rejection has stirred up.

I make my way back to the town square, my mind churning. How can anyone choose to stay stuck in the past like that? Doesn't Oliver see that he's dooming his business to failure by clinging to outdated methods?

As I pass the courthouse, I notice a flyer posted on the community bulletin board. "Benton Falls High

School Jazz Band Holiday Concert - Tonight at 7:30 PM." it proclaims in cheery red and green letters.

I'm about to walk past when I hear a familiar voice behind me. "Oh, Chloe. Are you thinking of going to the concert?"

I turn to find Rebecca, the neighbor from yesterday, beaming at me. Her golden hair is tucked under a fuzzy white hat, and her cheeks are pink from the cold. She looks like she's stepped right out of a Christmas card, all youthful beauty and holiday cheer.

"I... no, I was just reading the flyer," I stammer, caught off guard.

Rebecca's smile doesn't dim. "Oh, come on. I hear the jazz band is fantastic, and it's such a wonderful way to get into the holiday spirit. Plus, I hear Oliver Hanks will be there—he always brings hot chocolate for everyone."

At the mention of Oliver's name, I feel a renewed surge of irritation. "I'm afraid I have too much work to do," I say stiffly. "Enjoy the concert."

I start to walk away, but Rebecca's next words stop me in my tracks. "You know, sometimes the best way to solve a problem is to step away from it for a while. Music has a way of clearing the mind."

I turn back, startled by her insight. How does she know I'm grappling with a problem? I study her face, searching for any sign of insincerity or hidden motives. Her smile is warm and inviting, but there's something in her eyes - a flicker of... what? Judgment? Pity? I can't quite place it, but it leaves me feeling unsettled.

"I'll... think about it," I say noncommittally.

Rebecca's smile widens. "I hope to see you there, Chloe. It would be nice to get to know you better."

As she walks away, I can't shake the feeling that despite her friendly words, Rebecca doesn't really like me. It's a ridiculous thought - we've barely interacted. But there's something about her perfect demeanor, her effortless charm, that makes me feel like I'm being measured and found wanting.

I shake my head, trying to clear these paranoid thoughts. I don't need the approval of some small-town girl, no matter how pretty or popular she might be.

Still, as I make my way back to the house, Rebecca's words about the concert linger in my mind. The rational part of my brain is screaming at me to go back to the house, to bury myself in work—if I can find any—and forget this strange, frustrating day. But a smaller, quieter part—a part I thought I'd silenced long ago—whispers that maybe, just maybe, a change of scenery might help.

With a sigh of resignation, I check my watch. 6:30 PM. I have just enough time to go back to the house and change before the concert.

An hour later, I slip into the back row of the high school auditorium, the sounds of students tuning their instruments filling the air. The space is packed, the excited chatter of parents and community members creating a buzz of anticipation.

I spot Oliver near the front, distributing cups of steaming hot chocolate. He moves with purpose, his broad shoulders easily parting the crowd as he makes his way through the room. Our eyes meet for a brief moment, and I see a flicker of surprise cross his face before he gives me a curt nod and turns back to his task.

As the lights dim and the first notes of "Jingle Bell Rock" fill the air, I feel some of the tension leave my shoulders. The music is surprisingly good, the young musicians playing with a joy and enthusiasm that's infectious.

I find my foot tapping along to "Winter Wonderland," and by the time they launch into a jazzy rendition of "Silent Night," I'm actually... enjoying myself. The melodies wash over me, pushing away thoughts of apps and market shares and profit margins.

As the last notes of "We Wish You A Merry Christmas" fade away, I join in the applause, surprised by my enthusiasm. The students on stage beam with pride, and I feel an unexpected lump in my throat as I watch their parents rush forward to congratulate them.

As the crowd disperses, I make my way towards the exit, my mind whirling with new thoughts and possibilities. I'm so lost in my musings that I nearly collide with someone in the doorway.

"Whoa there." A familiar deep voice says, a firm hand steadying me. I look up to find Oliver looking down at me, his expression a mix of surprise and amusement. "Careful, Ms. Anderson. Wouldn't want you taking a spill."

"I... thank you," I mumble, flustered by his proximity

and the lingering effect of the music. "It was a good concert."

Oliver's eyebrows raise slightly. "High praise from the big city CEO. Didn't think this kind of thing would be your speed."

There's a challenge in his voice that sets my nerves on edge, and I find myself lifting my chin defiantly. "I'm full of surprises, Mr. Hanks. You shouldn't make assumptions about people based on first impressions."

A slow grin spreads across Oliver's face, and I'm struck by how it transforms his rugged features. "Fair enough," he says, his voice a low rumble. "Tell you what —why don't you stop by the store tomorrow? I'll give you the full Hanks' Department Store experience. No business talk, just good old-fashioned Christmas shopping. What do you say?"

I should say no. I should go back to the house and lose myself in work, forget this strange day and the even stranger feelings it's stirred up. But looking into Oliver's intense hazel eyes, feeling the warmth radiating from him in the chilly lobby, I nod.

"Alright, Mr. Hanks. You're on. But don't think this means I've given up on dragging your store into the modern age."

Oliver's grin widens, a glint of challenge in his eyes. "Wouldn't dream of it, Ms. Anderson. See you tomorrow."

As I step out into the chilly night air, snowflakes swirling around me, I feel... different. Lighter somehow, as if the music has washed away some of the hard shell I've built around myself over the years.

I know that tomorrow will bring new challenges, new frustrations. Oliver and I are still worlds apart in our views on business and life. But for tonight, walking home through the quiet, snow-covered streets of Benton Falls, I allow myself to simply exist in this moment. To feel the snowflakes melting on my cheeks, to hear the distant echo of Christmas carols, to remember what it's like to be part of something bigger than myself.

And for the first time since arriving in Benton Falls, I look forward to tomorrow, even as a small voice in the back of my mind warns me to be cautious. After all, in my experience, nothing good ever comes without a price.

Three

REBECCA

I appear back in heaven with a huff, my golden hair falling in my face as I stomp down the celestial pathway. Two days on Earth, and what do I have to show for it? A grumpy human who'd rather hug her laptop than a Christmas puppy. Ugh.

The pathway shimmers annoyingly beneath my feet, all pearly and perfect. I roll my eyes. Everything here is so disgustingly cheerful, it's like being stuck in a glitter factory. I can still smell the earthy scent of Benton Falls clinging to my clothes—a mix of pine, snow, and good old-fashioned human stubbornness.

As I march towards my apartment, all I can think about is Chloe Anderson and her stupid, perfect hair. Who does she think she is, anyway? Miss High-and-Mighty CEO with her designer suits and her "I'm too important for Christmas" attitude. It's like looking in a mirror, and let me tell you, I do not like what I see.

"Well, well, if it isn't our celestial weathergirl." A

voice calls out, dripping with sarcasm. Great. Just what I need.

I turn to see Gina, another angel-in-training, who lives a couple of doors down from me. She smirks at me. "How's the forecast looking, Rebecca? Cloudy with a chance of failure?"

I paste on my fakest smile. "Oh, you know, just peachy. How's the view from up there on your high horse?"

Gina's smirk falters for a second before she recovers. "Better than being earthbound. Have fun with your little human project." She grins, "And don't worry, you can always try again in 100 years." Gina saunters off, leaving me seething.

I kick at a celestial flower, immediately feeling guilty as it chimes sadly. "Sorry," I mutter, before remembering I'm talking to a flower. This place is making me lose it. I don't know how someone like Gina even qualifies to attend the Institute. I know we're not all guardian angels just yet, but I thought you had to at least be somewhat nice.

"Tough day at the office?"

I jump, spinning around to find Henry standing there, his silver hair aglow. How does he always manage to sneak up on me?

"Henry." I exclaim, trying to compose myself. "I was just... uh..."

"Taking out your frustrations on the local flora?" He raises an eyebrow, eyes twinkling with amusement.

I deflate, shoulders slumping. "Is it that obvious?"

Henry chuckles, the sound reminding me of my grandpa's old truck engine. "Only to someone who's been watching you mope down the path for the last five minutes. Come on, let's take a walk."

I follow him, dragging my feet like a sulky teenager. We end up at the Celestial Sea, which is doing its usual show-off routine with swirling colors and a sunset that belongs on a postcard. We sit on a bench that looks like it's made of tangled Christmas lights.

"So," Henry says, "how's our friend Chloe doing?"

I groan, flopping back dramatically. "She's impossible. I decorated her whole house, Henry. The whole thing. Lights, tree, garlands - the works. And you know what she did? She looked at it like I'd filled her living room with manure."

Henry's eyebrows shoot up. "You decorated her entire house?"

"Well, yeah," I say, suddenly feeling a bit sheepish. "Go big or go home, right? I thought it might, I don't know, shock her into feeling Christmassy or something."

Henry's silent for a moment, and then he laughs. Not just a chuckle, but a full-on, belly-shaking laugh that makes the nearby flowers start chiming in harmony.

"Oh, Rebecca," he wheezes, wiping tears from his eyes. "You certainly don't do anything by halves, do you?"

I cross my arms, pouting. "Well, what was I supposed to do? She's allergic to joy, I swear. I invited her to the tree lighting ceremony, and you'd think I'd asked her to go dumpster diving."

Henry's laughter subsides, but his eyes are still crinkled with amusement. "And how does that make you feel?"

"Frustrated. Annoyed. Like I want to shake her until jingle bells fall out." I throw my hands up in exasperation. "She's just so... so..."

"Like you used to be?" Henry suggests gently.

I freeze, the words hitting me like a snowball in the face. "I... that's not... I mean..."

But even as I try to deny it, I know he's right. Chloe's drive, her focus on success, her dismissal of anything that doesn't fit into her master plan—it's all painfully familiar.

"Okay, fine," I admit grudgingly. "She might be a teeny tiny bit like I used to be. But that's why this will never work. How am I supposed to help her when I'm still trying to figure this stuff out for myself? In case you haven't noticed, I'm not exactly Miss Christmas Spirit over here."

Henry nods thoughtfully. "And why do you think that is?"

I shrug, picking at a loose thread on my robe. "I don't know. I guess... I'm scared? What if I can't do this, Henry? What if I fail and I'm stuck being the weather girl for eternity? Do you know how boring it is to forecast 'sunny and perfect' every single day?"

Henry's hand comes to rest on my shoulder, warm

and comforting. "Rebecca, my dear, has it occurred to you that perhaps this assignment isn't just about Chloe?"

I look at him, confused. "What do you mean?"

"Sometimes, the best way to learn is by teaching," he says softly. "In helping Chloe discover the true spirit of Christmas, you might just rediscover it yourself."

And just like that, my chances of passing this assignment just decreased by 50%.

"So, what should I do?" I ask, feeling small and uncertain. "How do I help her when I'm still so messed up myself?"

Henry smiles, his entire face lighting up. "By being genuine. By showing her it's okay to be imperfect, to struggle, to learn. Share your own journey with her, Rebecca. Let her see that change is possible, that there's joy in the process of growth."

I nod slowly, a plan forming in my mind. "So, no more sneaky decorating?"

Henry chuckles. "Perhaps ease up on the grand gestures. Focus on the small things—a kind word, a moment of understanding. Sometimes the biggest changes start with the tiniest actions."

As we stand to leave, I feel a little lighter, a little more hopeful. Maybe, just maybe, I can do this.

"Oh, and Rebecca?" Henry calls as we part ways. "Remember, you have resources at your disposal. Your empathy, your intuition, even the Blessing Hotline if you need it. Use them wisely."

I nod, a small smile tugging at my lips. "Thanks, Henry. For everything."

As I walk back to my apartment, I actually notice the beauty around me for once. The star-speckled sky, the soft glow of the pearly buildings, even the annoyingly cheerful flowers. It's all pretty amazing when you stop to look.

I flop onto my cloud-soft bed, my mind buzzing with ideas for tomorrow. No more over-the-top schemes. Just me, being real, trying to connect with Chloe human-to-former-human. Who knows? Maybe in helping Chloe find her Christmas spirit, I'll find mine too.

And hey, if all else fails, at least it beats forecasting eternal sunshine.

Four

CHLOE

I stand before the grand entrance of Hanks' Department Store, my hand hovering over the brass doorknob. The morning air nips at my cheeks, and snowflakes dance around me, dusting my dark hair with tiny crystals that sparkle in the early sunlight. Despite the cold, there's a warmth to this town that I can't quite shake off, no matter how hard I try.

The store's large frosted windows showcase elaborate holiday displays that would put any big city store to shame. Vintage toys, twinkling lights, and festive garlands create miniature winter wonderlands that have a small crowd of children pressed against the glass, their eyes wide with wonder.

Taking a deep breath, I push open the heavy wooden door. The cheerful jingle of bells announces my arrival, and I'm immediately enveloped in a cocoon of warmth and the rich scent of cloves and oranges. The interior of the store is even more of a throwback than the outside, with high ceilings adorned with ornate moldings and brass chandeliers casting a warm glow over the merchandise.

Wooden display tables are laden with carefully arranged holiday gifts, everything from plush toys to fine scarves, all wrapped in bright, festive paper. A grand staircase, its banister wrapped in evergreen garlands and twinkling lights, leads to a second floor that promises even more wares.

"Well, look who's back," a deep voice calls out, tinged with amusement. I turn to see Oliver Hanks approaching, a box of ornaments in his arms. His sandy hair is charmingly disheveled, and his hazel eyes sparkle with good humor. "I wasn't sure you'd come. Couldn't stay away from our old-fashioned charm, Ms. Anderson?"

I feel a smile tugging at my lips despite myself. "Just thought I'd see if you've come to your senses about modernizing, Mr. Hanks."

Oliver chuckles, setting down the box on a nearby counter. "Still beating that drum, huh? Well, I hate to disappoint you, but we're still as delightfully outdated as ever."

As he speaks, I can't help but notice the way his eyes crinkle at the corners when he smiles, or how his rolled-up sleeves reveal muscular forearms dusted with a light tan. There's something undeniably attractive about a man who works with his hands, a thought I quickly push aside.

"Well, since I'm here," I say, trying to regain my professional composure, "at your invitation, perhaps you could show me around? I'd like to see how this... traditional approach of yours works in practice."

Oliver's eyebrows shoot up in surprise, but his smile widens. "I'd be happy to give you the grand tour, Ms. Anderson. Though I warn you, it might just change your mind about the value of a personal touch."

As we move through the store, I'm struck by how different it feels from the slick, efficient retail spaces I'm used to. Here, every item seems to have a story, every display a personal touch. Oliver introduces me to his employee, Sam, who is busy arranging an assortment of garish Christmas socks and continues to greet each customer by name, asking after their families or commenting on recent town events.

"Mrs. Johnson." he calls out to an older woman examining a display of hand-knit scarves. "How's that granddaughter of yours doing at college?"

Mrs. Johnson's face lights up. "Oh, Oliver, she's doing wonderfully. Just made the Dean's list. I was actually looking for something special to send her as a congratulations gift."

Oliver nods thoughtfully. "I think I have just the thing." He leads her to a display of delicate, hand-painted ornaments. "These just came in from a local artist. Each one's unique, just like your Milly."

I watch in fascination as Mrs. Johnson coos over the ornaments, finally selecting one that, according to Oliver, "has Milly's spirit." The entire interaction takes nearly fifteen minutes—wildly inefficient by my standards, but I can't deny the genuine joy on Mrs. Johnson's face as she leaves the store, her purchase carefully wrapped in tissue paper and nestled in a festive bag.

"You see," Oliver says, turning to me with a knowing smile, "that's something you can't replicate with an app or an online store. That personal connection, the ability to really understand what each customer needs and wants—that's the heart of Hanks' Department Store."

I nod slowly, beginning to understand. "But surely there must be ways to streamline your operations without losing that personal touch? I mean, just keeping track of inventory alone must be a nightmare."

Oliver's smile falters slightly, and for the first time, I notice the shadows under his eyes, the slight slump in his shoulders. "Well, I won't pretend it's not challenging," he admits. "But we manage. The important thing is keeping the spirit of the store alive."

Before I can press further, the bell over the door jingles merrily, and a familiar voice calls out, "Hello. I brought some homemade gingerbread."

I turn to see Rebecca breezing into the store with a festive tin in her hands. Her golden hair is frosted with snowflakes, and her cheeks are pink from the cold. She stops short when she sees me, her eyes widening in surprise.

"Oh. Chloe, I didn't expect to see you here," she says, her smile bright and genuine? "Are you doing some Christmas shopping?"

"Just getting to know the local businesses," I reply, studying her carefully. There's something about Rebecca that doesn't quite add up, but I can't put my finger on what it is.

"Me too." Rebecca smiles. Whatever I thought I noticed yesterday seems to be gone. Perhaps she does like me. "Thought I'd deliver some Christmas goodies to the local shops."

Oliver looks at us, confusion clear on his face. "You two know each other?"

"We're neighbors," I explain, watching as Rebecca's smile falters for just a moment. "Rebecca introduced herself when I arrived in town."

"Oh," Oliver says, still looking puzzled. "That's... nice. Though I must admit, I don't think I've seen you around before. Are you new in town?"

Rebecca laughs, a tinkling sound that seems almost too perfect. "Oh, you know how it is in small towns. Easy to overlook people. I've been here... well, it feels like forever, really."

I narrow my eyes, my suspicions growing. How could Oliver, who seems to know every person in Benton Falls by name, not recognize Rebecca?

Before I can voice my doubts, Rebecca thrusts the tin of gingerbread into Oliver's hands. "Anyway, I should be going. Lots of holiday cheer to spread. Enjoy the gingerbread. And Chloe... it was nice to see you again."

With that, she's gone in a swirl of golden hair and the lingering scent of gingerbread. Oliver and I stand in silence for a moment, both seemingly unsure of what had just happened.

"Well," Oliver finally says, opening the tin, "at least

the gingerbread smells amazing. Would you like a piece, Chloe?"

The use of my first name startles me, but I find I don't mind it coming from him. "Sure, why not?" I say, reaching for a perfectly shaped gingerbread man.

As I bite into the cookie, the rich flavors of molasses, cinnamon, and clove explode on my tongue. It's possibly the best gingerbread I've ever tasted, and for a moment, I'm transported back to childhood Christmases, to a time before success and money became my sole focus.

"This is… really good," I admit, surprised by how much I'm enjoying it.

Oliver nods, a wistful expression on his face. "It reminds me of the gingerbread my mom used to make. She'd bake dozens of cookies every Christmas, and we'd spend hours decorating them as a family."

There's a warmth in his voice, a depth of emotion that catches me off guard. "That sounds… nice," I say, unsure how to respond to such an open display of sentiment.

Oliver seems to shake himself out of his reverie. "It was. But hey, that's what Christmas is all about, right? Creating those kinds of memories, spreading joy to others."

I nod noncommittally, but inside, I'm conflicted. The warmth and genuine happiness I see in Oliver's eyes as he talks about family and traditions stir something in me, a longing I thought I'd buried long ago.

As we continue our tour of the store, I pay more attention to the customers, to the way they interact with

Oliver and his staff. There's a sense of community here, of belonging, that I've never experienced in my world of boardrooms and business deals.

We're examining a display of handcrafted ornaments when I notice Oliver's shoulders slump slightly. "These are beautiful," I say, picking up a delicate glass snowflake. "But they must be expensive to stock."

Oliver nods, a shadow passing over his face. "They are. And to be honest, they're not selling as well as I'd hoped. With the new big box store that opened on the outskirts of town, we've been struggling to compete on price."

I feel a pang of sympathy, surprising myself. "That must be difficult," I say softly.

Oliver shrugs, trying to put on a brave face. "We'll manage. We always do. The store's been through tough times before."

But I can see the worry in his eyes, the slight tremor in his hands as he carefully rearranges the ornaments. For the first time, I understand the actual cost of maintaining this old-fashioned approach to business.

"Oliver," I say hesitantly, "have you considered... I mean, there are ways to modernize your operations that could help cut costs without losing the personal touch. My app, for instance—"

Oliver holds up a hand, his expression a mix of gratitude and resignation. "I appreciate the thought, Chloe, I really do. But Hanks' Department Store isn't just a business. It's a piece of Benton Falls history, a legacy my grandfather started. I can't just change everything to chase profits."

I want to argue, to explain how he could preserve the store's character while still turning a profit, but the look in Oliver's eyes stops me. There's a determination there, a belief in something greater than just the bottom line, that I find both admirable and frustrating.

As we make our way back to the front of the store, I'm struck by the contrast between Oliver's financial worries and the joy he clearly finds in his work. He stops to help a young boy pick out a gift for his mother, spending several minutes crouched down at the child's level, listening intently to his thoughts on what his mom might like.

The scene stirs something in me, a memory of my own mother, of the few precious Christmases we had together before she passed away. I remember the way her eyes would light up at the simplest gifts, how she always said it was the thought that counted.

For the first time in years, I question my beliefs about money and happiness. I've always equated financial success with security, with worth. But watching Oliver, seeing the genuine connections he forms with his customers and the pride he takes in his work, I wonder if I've been missing something all along.

As the day winds down and the last customer leaves the store, Oliver turns to me with a tired but genuine smile. "Well, Ms. Anderson, what's the verdict? Have we managed to sway you to the charms of old-fashioned retail?"

I laugh softly, surprised by how much I've enjoyed the day. "I'll admit, there's something special about this place. But I still think there are ways you could improve your operations without losing that charm."

Oliver nods, his expression thoughtful. "Maybe you're right. I suppose I've been so focused on preserving the past that I have given little thought to the future."

We stand in silence for a moment, the soft glow of Christmas lights reflecting off the polished wood counters. I'm acutely aware of Oliver's presence beside me, of the warmth radiating from him in the quiet store.

"Thank you for today," I say finally, surprised by the sincerity in my voice. "It's given me a lot to think about."

Oliver's smile widens, reaching his eyes and making them crinkle at the corners. "Well, that works both ways, Chloe. You've certainly given me some food for thought as well."

As I prepare to leave, bundling up against the cold night air, Oliver hesitates, then says, "Benton Falls really shines at Christmas. A lot of fun things to do. Maybe I'll see you around?"

I pause, my hand on the door. My first instinct is to decline, to retreat to the safety of my grandmother's house and my familiar world of spreadsheets and profit margins. But something stops me—the memory of Oliver's kindness, the warmth of the store, the unexpected joy I found in simply being part of something larger than myself.

"Uh... maybe you will," I say finally, offering Oliver a small smile.

Stepping out into the chilly night air, snowflakes swirling around me, I look back at the store. Through the frosted windows, I can see Oliver moving about, straightening displays and tidying up. The sight stirs something in me, a warmth that has nothing to do with the cozy interior of the store.

Walking home through the quiet, snow-covered streets of Benton Falls, I can't shake the feeling that something has shifted inside me. The twinkling lights of the houses I pass, the distant sound of carols drifting from an open window, even the crunch of snow beneath my feet—it all seems somehow more vibrant, more alive.

And as I reach my grandmother's house, the Christmas lights twinkling merrily in welcome, I realize that maybe, just maybe, there's more to life than balance sheets and profit margins.

Maybe, somewhere between the shelves of Hanks' Department Store and the snowy streets of Benton Falls, I've begun to rediscover a part of myself I thought was long lost. A part that remembers the joy of giving, the warmth of community, and the magic of Christmas.

As I unlock the door and step into the warmth of the house, I hum a Christmas carol under my breath. And for once, I don't try to stop myself.

Five

CHLOE

The gentle crackle of the fireplace fills the living room of my grandmother's house, casting a warm glow that dances across the walls. Outside, snowflakes drift lazily past the window, adding to the thick blanket of white already covering the ground. It's the perfect setting for a cozy evening, but the earlier contentment I'd arrived home with is gone; replaced by an uneasy, gnawing feeling. Oliver's store and his small town rose-colored glasses aren't real life.

I stare at my laptop screen, the figures on my latest project blurring before my eyes. My mind keeps wandering back to yesterday's visit to Hanks' Department Store, to Oliver's kind eyes and the warmth of his smile. The memory of his financial struggles tugs at something inside me, a feeling I'm not comfortable with.

With a frustrated sigh, I slam my laptop shut and push it away. This isn't like me. I don't worry about small-town shopkeepers or get caught up in sentimental holiday nonsense. I make smart, calculated decisions based on facts and figures, not feelings.

"Get it together, Chloe," I mutter to myself, standing up to pace the room. The plush carpet muffles my footsteps, but it can't quiet the turmoil in my head.

I catch a glimpse of myself in the mirror above the fireplace. My dark hair is slightly disheveled, and there's a softness in my eyes that I don't recognize. It's only been a few days, and I can feel myself reverting to the lonely girl I used to be, no matter how much Christmas cheer I'm being dosed with. I've worked too hard, built too many walls to let them crumble now.

The memory of my childhood rises unbidden. There were only a few years with my parents and then such a short time with my grandmother, a brief respite of love and stability... only to have it ripped away when she passed. Then came the constant moves, the pitying looks from teachers and classmates, the ache of never quite belonging. The pain of loss and the ache of loneliness still feel raw, even after all these years.

No, I decide, squaring my shoulders and meeting my reflection's gaze. I can't let myself be vulnerable again. Money is safe. Success is safe. Caring about people, getting involved in their lives—that's a one-way ticket to heartbreak.

I march over to my phone, determined to book the first flight out of here tomorrow. Just as I'm about to dial, a knock at the door interrupts me.

For a moment, I consider ignoring it. But curiosity gets the better of me, and I open the door to find

Rebecca standing on the porch, wearing a bright green beanie, her hair in a braid falling across her shoulder.

"Chloe, I'm so glad I caught you," she says, her smile bright enough to rival the Christmas lights adorning the porch. "I wanted to invite you to the Live Nativity Scene at the church tonight. It's a real Benton Falls tradition."

I open my mouth to refuse, but something stops me. Maybe it's the earnest look in Rebecca's eyes, or maybe it's the realization that this might be my last night in this town. Either way, I say, "Actually, that might be nice. I was thinking of leaving town tomorrow, so this could be a good way to say goodbye to Benton Falls."

Rebecca's smile falters for a moment, but she quickly recovers. "Leaving? Oh, but you just got here. Well, all the more reason for you to come tonight then. I promise, it'll be magical."

I nod, suddenly feeling a strange mix of relief and regret. "Alright, let me just grab my coat."

As we walk towards the church, the sound of our boots crunching in the snow is accompanied by the distant chiming of bells. The air is fresh and clean, carrying the scent of fresh snow and wood smoke. Despite myself, I feel a sense of peace settling over me.

"So," Rebecca says, breaking the comfortable silence, "what made you decide to leave so soon?"

I shrug, trying to keep my tone casual. "Oh, you know. Work never stops. I've got a company to run."

Rebecca nods, but there's a knowing look in her eyes that makes me uncomfortable. "I understand. But sometimes, taking a step back can give us a new perspective on what's really important."

Before I can respond, we turn a corner, and the church comes into view. The colonial building stands proud against the night sky, its red brick façade and white trim illuminated by soft lighting. Two majestic oak trees flank the cobblestone path leading to the entrance, their bare branches reaching towards the stars.

As we approach, I can hear the gentle strains of "Silent Night" floating in the air. The courtyard is transformed into a living tableau of the nativity scene, complete with costumed actors and live animals. The soft glow of lanterns casts a warm light over the scene, creating an atmosphere of reverence and wonder.

"It's beautiful," I whisper, surprised by the lump forming in my throat.

Rebecca smiles, gently guiding me closer. "Wait until you see everyone come together. It's not just about the scene—it's about the community."

We join the gathering crowd, and I'm struck by the sense of warmth and belonging that seems to envelop everyone. Children giggle softly as they pet the docile sheep, while elderly couples stand hand in hand, their faces glowing with nostalgia and joy.

I spot Oliver among the crowd, dressed as one of the shepherds. Our eyes meet, and he gives me a warm smile that sends an unexpected flutter through my chest. I quickly look away, reminding myself of my decision to leave.

The performance begins, and I find myself drawn

into the timeless story. The young couple playing Mary and Joseph bring a touching sincerity to their roles, and the live animals add an element of unpredictability that keeps everyone engaged.

As the story unfolds, I notice something else happening around me. People are quietly helping each other—offering blankets to those who look cold, sharing thermoses of hot cocoa, assisting an older man to a better viewing spot. It's a subtle choreography of kindness that seems as much a part of the event as the nativity scene itself.

During a quiet moment in the performance, Rebecca leans in and whispers, "See that woman over there, handing out programs? She runs the local food bank. And the man playing Joseph? He organizes the food pantry to help the less fortunate."

I look around with fresh eyes, suddenly seeing beyond the costumes and pageantry. These aren't just townspeople playing roles—they're individuals who have woven their lives together into a tapestry of community and mutual support.

A memory surfaces—my grandmother, her eyes twinkling as she helped me wrap presents for her church's giving tree. "Christmas isn't about what we get, Chloe," she had said. "It's about what we give."

I feel a tightness in my chest, a mixture of longing and something else I can't quite name. For a moment, I allow myself to imagine being part of something like this —not just an observer, but a participant in this web of care and connection.

As the performance reaches its climax, with the wise men bearing gifts, I blink back unexpected tears. The simple beauty of the scene, the palpable sense of community spirit—it's all so far removed from the world I've built for myself, and yet... it feels like coming home.

The last notes of "Joy to the World" fade away, replaced by the sound of applause and cheerful chatter as the crowd disperses. I stand rooted to the spot, overwhelmed by emotions I'm not sure how to process.

Rebecca touches my arm gently. "Are you okay, Chloe?"

I nod, not trusting my voice. As we walk back towards my grandmother's house, the cold air helps clear my head a little.

"It was... nice," I finally manage, knowing the word is woefully inadequate to describe what I've just experienced.

Rebecca smiles knowingly. "It's more than nice, isn't it? It's a reminder of what Christmas is really about—love, community, giving."

I nod again, my mind whirling. Everything I've seen tonight goes against the carefully constructed worldview I've built over the years. That true wealth might be measured in relationships rather than dollars, that vulnerability could be a strength rather than a weakness—it's all so foreign, and yet... oddly appealing.

As we reach my front porch, Rebecca turns to me. "So, are you still planning to leave tomorrow?"

I hesitate, my earlier determination wavering. "I... I'm not sure. I need to think about some things."

Rebecca's smile is warm and understanding. "That's okay. Sometimes the best decisions come after a good night's sleep. Whatever you choose, Chloe, just know that you have a place here in Benton Falls, if you want it."

With a final goodnight, Rebecca heads off into the snowy night, leaving me alone with my thoughts. I unlock the door and step inside. The warmth of the house wraps around me like a hug.

After I hang up my coat, my eyes fall on a framed photo of my grandmother that I hadn't really noticed before. She's standing in front of Hanks' Department Store, her arms full of gift-wrapped packages, her face alight with joy. The sight stirs something deep inside me, a longing for connection that I've kept buried for far too long.

I sink onto the couch, my head in my hands. The walls I've built around my heart, the ones I was so determined to reinforce just hours ago, suddenly feel more like a prison than a protection. But the thought of tearing them down, of allowing myself to care, to be vulnerable —it's terrifying.

As I sit there, wrestling with my conflicting emotions, a soft 'ping' from my phone catches my attention. It's an email notification from a client—followed by another gently worded reminder from my board of directors that they've got things covered. I'm not so sure. My company is the only thing I've got.

The familiar pull of duty and ambition tugs at me, offering the comforting familiarity of spreadsheets and profit margins. It would be so easy to go back, to insist I only needed a few days to unwind, leave Benton Falls and it's unsettling influence behind.

But as I reach for my phone, my eyes once again fall on the photo of my grandmother. I remember her words about the true meaning of Christmas, about the importance of giving. I think about Oliver's dedication to his store and his community, about the way the townspeople came together at the nativity scene.

With a deep breath, I make a decision. I won't book a flight—not yet. I'll give Benton Falls one more day.

Lying in bed, I stare up at the ceiling, my mind replaying scenes from the evening—the gentle lowing of the cattle in the manger, the look of wonder on children's faces, the warmth in Oliver's eyes as he caught sight of me in the crowd.

For the first time in years, I allow myself to imagine a different life. One where I have family and friends who love me, one where success is measured not just in dollars and cents, but in the strength of relationships and the impact on a community.

As I drift off to sleep, the last thing I see in my mind's eye is the nativity scene, bathed in gentle light. But now, instead of being a mere observer, I see myself as part of it —not playing a role, but simply being present, connected, belonging.

It's been a while since I've felt like I've belonged to anything but my company in a long time.

Six

REBECCA

The frosty December air bites at my cheeks as I stand on Chloe's porch, my hand poised to knock. Even though I don't actually feel cold (perks of being an angel-in-training), I pull my coat tighter around me, trying to look as human as possible. The scent of pine and orange wafts from a nearby wreath, mingling with the earthier smell of wood smoke from the chimney. It's so different from the perpetual perfection of heaven's atmosphere—a bit messy, sure, but undeniably alive.

Taking a deep breath, I plaster on my best "friendly neighbor" smile and knock on the door. It's December 9th and there isn't time to waste if I plan on completing my assignment by Christmas Eve. Gratefully, Chloe hasn't mentioned leaving since Sunday—crisis averted—and it's time to move forward.

After a moment, I hear footsteps approaching, and then the door swings open to reveal Chloe. Her dark hair is perfectly styled, and she's wearing a designer sweater that probably costs more than most people's entire wardrobes.

"Rebecca," she says, surprise and a hint of wariness in her voice. "What are you doing here?"

I beam at her, channeling all the Christmas cheer I can muster. "I'm here to escort you to the community caroling night."

Chloe's eyebrow arches skeptically. "I don't recall agreeing to attend any caroling night."

"Oh, come on," I wheedle, trying not to let my desperation show. "It's a Benton Falls tradition. You can't spend Christmas here without experiencing it at least once."

She crosses her arms, looking unimpressed. "The jazz band concert was enough, not to mention the live nativity. I'm not much for singing. Or crowds. Or standing in the cold for no good reason."

I feel a flash of irritation. This woman is more difficult than I expected. But then I remember Henry's words about patience and empathy. I take a moment to reach out with my angelic senses, trying to understand what Chloe's really feeling beneath her prickly exterior.

The emotions hit me like a wave—loneliness, fear, a deep-seated longing for connection, that she's trying desperately to ignore. Must be an angel thing because my heart softens. No wonder she's so resistant to the Christmas spirit.

"It's not about the singing, really," I whisper. "It's about being part of something bigger than yourself. Plus, I heard Oliver might be there..."

I see a flicker of interest in Chloe's eyes at the mention of Oliver's name. Bingo.

She sighs heavily, as if I'm asking her to climb Mount Everest rather than attend a festive community event. "Fine. I'll go for a little while, which has nothing to do with Oliver. But I'm not singing."

"Deal." I chirp, resisting the urge to do a celestial happy dance on her porch.

Fifteen minutes later, we're walking towards the town square. The sound of our boots crunching in the snow is accompanied by the distant chiming of bells. Chloe is silent beside me, her posture stiff and her hands shoved deep into her coat pockets. She's got to be miserable in those high-heeled boots.

As we round the corner, the full splendor of the caroling night comes into view. The courthouse clock tower is adorned with twinkling lights, casting a warm glow over the gathering crowd. The massive Christmas tree in the center of the square is heavy with ornaments, its lights reflecting off the snow. The air is filled with the smell of hot cocoa and the sound of cheerful chatter.

I sneak a glance at Chloe and see her eyes widening slightly as she takes it all in.

"It's something, isn't it?" I say softly.

She nods, seemingly despite herself. "It's... picturesque," she admits grudgingly.

As we make our way into the crowd, I point out various townspeople to Chloe, spinning stories about their lives and contributions to the community. It's a risky move—I'm essentially making things up based on what I can glean from my angelic intuition—but I need Chloe to see the heart of this town.

"See that group over there?" I gesture towards a cluster of elderly ladies, their white hair peeking out from beneath colorful knit hats. "They make care packages for the troops. And those teenagers by the tree? They organize the Secret Santa program at the school."

Chloe's brow furrows. "How do you know all this?"

I shrug, trying to look nonchalant. "Oh, you know how small towns are. Everyone knows everyone's business."

Before Chloe can question me further, I spot Oliver making his way through the crowd, distributing flyers. "Oh look, there's Oliver." I say, perhaps a bit too enthusiastically. "Let's go say hi."

I gently steer Chloe in Oliver's direction, ignoring her protests. As we approach, Oliver looks up, his face breaking into a warm smile that makes his eyes crinkle at the corners.

"Chloe, I'm so glad you could make it," he says, his voice full of genuine pleasure. "And Rebecca, always a pleasure."

I beam at him, noting the way Chloe's posture straightens ever so slightly in Oliver's presence. Oh, this is too perfect.

If ever there was a way to get a woman to do something crazy, like get into the season of giving, a hot guy is the answer. I'm not sure why I didn't think of this as my ace in the hole until now—probably because angels aren't supposed to play poker.

"Oliver was just telling me about the toy drive the other day," I say, nudging Chloe gently. "It sounds like such a wonderful initiative."

Chloe shoots me a look that could freeze hell over, but I just smile innocently. Come on, Chloe. Take the bait.

After a moment of awkward silence, Chloe finally speaks. "A toy drive? That sounds... nice. How does it work?"

Oliver's face lights up like the Christmas tree behind him as he launches into an explanation of the toy drive. I watch with satisfaction as Chloe listens, her initial reluctance giving way to genuine interest.

"The only problem," Oliver says, his enthusiasm dimming slightly, "is that I'm struggling a bit with the logistics of it all. Tracking donations, organizing distribution... it's more complicated than I expected."

I can practically see the gears turning in Chloe's head. "That sounds challenging," she says slowly. "Have you considered using a digital inventory system? It could streamline the entire process."

Oliver's eyes widen. "I hadn't even thought of that. Chloe, that's brilliant."

As the two of them discuss the possibilities, I take a small step back, feeling a warm glow of accomplishment. Mission accomplished, for now at least.

Just then, a hush falls over the crowd as the mayor steps up to the lectern in front of the Christmas tree. "Ladies and gentlemen," he announces, his voice booming across the square, "it's time for our annual community caroling to begin."

A cheer goes up from the crowd, and I notice Chloe shifting uncomfortably. "Maybe we should go," she mutters to me. "I told you, I'm not much of a singer."

"Oh, come on," I insist, gently taking her arm. "You don't have to sing if you don't want to. Just stay and listen. Please?"

She hesitates, and I can sense her internal struggle. Part of her wants to flee back to the safety of her grandmother's house, but another part—a part she's trying hard to ignore – is drawn to the warmth and camaraderie of the gathering.

I've been there before.

Finally, she sighs. "Fine. We'll stay for a little while."

Victory. I guide her towards the edge of the crowd where we can observe without feeling too overwhelmed. Oliver joins us, standing close enough to Chloe that their shoulders almost touch.

As the first strains of "Deck the Halls" fill the air, I watch Chloe's face carefully. Her expression remains neutral, but I can sense a softening in her energy. By the time we get to "Silent Night," I notice her foot tapping ever so slightly to the rhythm.

The caroling continues, the harmonies of the townspeople rising into the night sky. I close my eyes for a moment, letting the music wash over me. It's different from the perfect, angelic choirs of heaven – a bit rough around the edges, with the occasional off-key note – but there's a warmth and sincerity to it that tugs at my heart.

When I open my eyes, I'm startled to see a tear glistening on Chloe's cheek. She quickly wipes it away, but not before I catch a glimpse of the raw emotion in her eyes.

"Are you okay?" I ask softly.

She nods, clearing her throat. "Fine. It's just... my grandmother used to love Christmas carols. We'd sing them together when I visited her here as a child."

My heart swells with compassion. "That sounds like a beautiful memory."

Chloe shrugs, her walls coming back up. "It was a long time ago."

As the caroling winds down, I notice Oliver gently touching Chloe's elbow. "I have to head out, but I was wondering... would you be interested in helping me set up the digital inventory system for the toy drive? Your expertise would be invaluable."

Chloe hesitates for a moment, then nods. "I suppose I could spare some time. For the children, of course."

Oliver's face breaks into a wide grin. "That's wonderful. Thank you, Chloe. This will make such a difference."

As Oliver says his goodbyes, I can't help but feel a surge of triumph. I've got Chloe involved in a charitable project and spending more time with Oliver. It's a good start, but I know I've got a long way to go before I can call this assignment a success.

Walking back to Chloe's house, I can sense a change in her mood. She's quieter, more thoughtful, and there's a softness in her eyes that wasn't there before.

"Thank you for dragging me out tonight," she says as we reach her porch. "It was... not entirely unpleasant."

I laugh, the sound tinkling like bells in the winter air. "High praise indeed. I'm glad you came, Chloe. Goodnight."

As I walk away, ostensibly towards my home, I can't help but feel a warm glow of accomplishment. It's a small step, but it's progress. Maybe, just maybe, I'm getting the hang of this guardian angel thing after all.

I find a quiet corner and prepare to go back home. Just before I disappear, I catch one last glimpse of Chloe standing on her porch, gazing out at the twinkling lights of Benton Falls with a contemplative expression.

A smile spreads across my face as the familiar tingle of celestial energy washes over me. Watch out, Chloe Anderson. Your guardian angel is just getting started.

Seven

CHLOE

The gentle hum of my laptop fills the cozy living room of my grandmother's house as I pore over spreadsheets and inventory lists. A cinnamon and fir candle is burning on the coffee table, a gift from Rebecca that I'd initially dismissed as overly festive but now find oddly comforting. Outside, snow falls softly, blanketing Benton Falls in a pristine white coat that sparkles in the sunlight.

I can't believe I've spent my day working on a toy drive, of all things. When I agreed to help Oliver at the community sing-along, I thought I'd just give him a few quick pointers and be done with it. But somehow—and thanks to Rebecca's early morning visit and a box full of toys, followed by a call from Oliver—I've found myself completely immersed in the project, determined to make it a success.

As I input another donation into the system, I catch myself smiling at the thought of a child's face lighting up on Christmas morning. The image catches me off guard, and I quickly shake it off. I'm doing this to help Oliver streamline his business practices, I remind myself sternly. Nothing more.

A knock at the door startles me from my thoughts. I open it to find Oliver standing on the porch, his arms laden with boxes and his cheeks ruddy from the cold.

"Afternoon, Chloe," he says with that warm smile that never fails to make my heart skip a beat—although I would never admit that to anyone. "I hope I'm not interrupting, but I've got some more donations for you to log."

I step aside to let him in, trying to ignore the flutter in my stomach as he brushes past me. "No interruption at all. I was just working on the inventory system."

Oliver sets the boxes down and looks around the room, his eyes twinkling. "Wow, you've really turned this place into command central, haven't you?"

I follow his gaze, suddenly seeing the room through his eyes. My laptop is surrounded by stacks of papers, sticky notes cover every available surface, and a large whiteboard I'd ordered online dominates one wall, covered in my neat handwriting detailing donation goals and distribution plans.

"I suppose I have," I admit, feeling a blush creep up my cheeks. "I just want to make sure everything's organized properly."

Oliver's smile softens as he surveys my work zone one more time. "How long have you been working on this?"

Shrugging, I close the door. "A few hours."

"It's amazing." He puts his hands in his pockets. "The kids of Benton Falls are lucky to have you on their side."

His words send a warm feeling spreading through my chest, one that I quickly try to squash. I'm not doing this for the kids, I tell myself. This is just a project, like any other.

"Yes, well," I say, clearing my throat. "Speaking of the toy drive, we should probably go through these new donations."

For the next hour, Oliver and I work side by side, sorting through the toys and logging them into the system I've created. As we work, Oliver regales me with stories about past toy drives and the children they've helped. Despite my best efforts to remain detached, I laugh at his jokes and hanging on every word.

"Oh, that reminds me," Oliver says suddenly, setting down a stuffed reindeer. "The high school band is having their holiday concert tonight. They always collect toy donations at the door. I know it's short notice, but would you like to come with me? You know, to oversee the donations and all that."

I hesitate. Sheesh, how many Christmas concerts can one town have? And suddenly I find my instinct to decline warring with an unexpected desire to say yes. "I don't know, Oliver. I'm not sure about another concert."

"Come on," his hazel eyes twinkling in persuasion. "It'll be fun. Plus, we'll be collecting donations. Who knows?" he beams. "You might even enjoy yourself."

I sigh, knowing I'm fighting a losing battle. "Fine. But only to oversee the donations."

Oliver's face breaks into a wide grin. "Great. I'll pick you up at seven."

As he leaves, I stand at the window, watching his retreating figure until it disappears into the snowy night. A small voice in the back of my mind whispers that I'm in danger of caring too much, of letting myself get too invested in this town and its people. But for once, I push that voice aside and worry about the most pressing problem—What am I going to wear?

Fifteen minutes later, I stand in front of the mirror, frowning at my reflection. I've changed outfits three times already, unsure of what to wear to a high school band concert in a small town. I finally settle on a soft cashmere sweater and dark jeans, a far cry from my usual power suits but somehow fitting for the occasion.

At precisely seven o'clock, there's a knock at the door. I open it to find Oliver standing there, looking handsome in a green sweater that brings out the flecks of gold in his eyes.

"Wow," he breathes, his gaze traveling over me. "You look beautiful, Chloe."

I feel a blush creeping up my cheeks, surprised at how much I appreciate his compliment. "Thank you. You don't look so bad yourself."

The drive to the high school is filled with comfortable conversation, punctuated by the soft strains of Christmas music from the radio. As we pull into the parking lot, I'm struck by the festive atmosphere. The school is decked out in twinkling lights, and families stream towards the entrance, many carrying wrapped gifts for the toy drive.

Inside the foyer is a hive of activity. A large Christmas tree dominates one corner, its branches laden with ornaments and twinkling lights. The evergreen scent mingles with the aroma of hot chocolate and freshly baked cookies being sold at a nearby table.

Oliver guides me to a table set up for toy donations, where we're greeted by an enthusiastic group of student volunteers. As we help them organize the incoming gifts, I'm surprised by how much I'm enjoying myself. The excited chatter of the students, the warmth of the community spirit, it all feels so... right.

Just as we're finishing up, Rebecca appears, her golden hair catching the light as she weaves through the crowd towards us.

"Chloe. Oliver. I'm so glad you're here," she says, her smile bright. "Isn't this wonderful? So many people have brought donations."

I nod, surprised to find that I actually agree with her. "It is pretty special," I admit.

Rebecca beams at me. "Oh, we should go in. The concert's about to start."

I nod and wonder how I seem to spend most of my time in Benton Falls with Rebecca, a girl I'm not totally convinced I really like. It's like she's got some weird agenda with me—like I'm her Christmas project.

Pushing the notion aside, we make our way into the auditorium, and I'm struck by the transformation. The stage has been turned into a winter wonderland, complete with sparkling fake snow and twinkling lights. The excitement in the air is palpable as parents and community members find their seats.

Oliver leads us to a row near the front, and I find myself sandwiched between him and Rebecca. As the lights dim and the first notes of "Rocking Around the Christmas Tree." fill the air, I'm surprised by the quality of the performance. These kids are good.

Throughout the concert, I find my foot tapping along to the music, a smile playing at my lips. During a moving rendition of "Silent Night," I feel Oliver's hand brush against mine on the armrest. Instead of pulling away, I let it stay there, enjoying the warmth of his touch.

As the last notes fade away and the applause dies down, I realize I've actually enjoyed myself. The joy on the faces of the students, the pride radiating from their parents, it all speaks to a sense of community that I've never experienced before.

"That was actually pretty great," I say to Oliver as we file out of the auditorium.

He grins at me. "I knew you'd enjoy it. Hey, want to grab a hot chocolate before we head out? I hear the PTA makes a mean peppermint cocoa."

I should say no. I should go home and get back to work. But the warmth in Oliver's eyes and the festive atmosphere around us make me throw caution to the wind. "Sure, why not?"

We make our way to the refreshment table, where Oliver insists on buying our drinks. As we sip our cocoa

—which is indeed delicious—we wander through the foyer, admiring the students' artwork displayed on the walls. Somewhere in the distance, we hear a crash.

Oliver turns to me. "We better go see if someone needs some help."

We head towards the noise and follow the crowd. A huge nutcracker had toppled over, and a woman was being attended to on the floor.

"That's Sadie," Oliver's voice is laced with concern. "She's our town librarian."

An older woman, with silver curls and blue eyes peering above her glasses, approaches us. "The ambulance is on its way. Don't worry, Officer Michaels has her."

Oliver lowers his chin and exhales, reassured by the information. "Thank you, Mrs. Henderson."

"I wonder what happened." Oliver puts his hand on the small of my back, gently guiding me away from the crowd. "But if Ren's there, I'm sure everything is under control."

"Who's Ren?" I move towards the donation table.

"One of our local police officers. He's a great guy."

This small town seems like it might fit in a snow globe, a world unto its own, where everyone seems to know and care about everyone. An itch manifests along my neck, scratching at the irritation. I think I might be allergic to this place.

"You know," Oliver says softly, "I'm really glad you came tonight, Chloe. And not just because of the toy drive. It's been nice spending time with you."

Instantly, the itch is gone, replaced by a soothing warmth that has nothing to do with the hot chocolate spreading through my chest. "I've enjoyed it too," I admit, surprising myself with my honesty.

Oliver's eyes meet mine, and for a moment, the bustling crowd around us fades away. I lean towards him almost involuntarily.

But then reality crashes back in. What am I doing? I'm leaving Benton Falls after the holidays. I can't let myself get attached, not to Oliver, not to this town, not to any of it.

I take a step back, clearing my throat. "We should probably start packing up the donations," I say, my voice sounding strained even to my own ears.

A flicker of disappointment crosses Oliver's face, but he nods. "You're right. Let's get to it."

As we work to box up the toys, a tense silence falls between us. I can feel Oliver's eyes on me, but I keep my focus on the task at hand, afraid of what I might do if I meet his gaze.

It's not until we're loading the last of the boxes into Oliver's truck that he speaks again. "Chloe," he says softly, "I hope I didn't make you uncomfortable back there. That wasn't my intention."

I sigh, finally looking up at him. The sincerity in his eyes makes my heart ache. "You didn't," I assure him. "It's just... I'm not staying in Benton Falls, Oliver. After the holidays, I'm going back to my real life. I can't... I can't let myself get too invested here."

Oliver nods slowly, but I can see the hurt in his eyes.

"I understand. But Chloe, have you considered that maybe this could be your real life? The way you've thrown yourself into the toy drive, the connections you're making here... it seems to me like you fit right in."

His words stir something in me, a longing I've been trying to ignore since I arrived in Benton Falls. But I shake my head, pushing it aside. "This isn't me, Oliver. The big city, the corporate world - that's where I belong."

"If you say so," he says, but I can tell he doesn't believe me. "Just... promise me you'll keep an open mind, okay? Benton Falls has a way of surprising people."

I nod, not trusting myself to speak. As Oliver drives me home, the silence between us is heavy with unspoken words and possibilities I'm too afraid to consider.

Back at my grandmother's house, I stand on the porch, watching Oliver's taillights disappear down the snowy street. The frosty night air nips at my cheeks, but I barely notice it, my mind whirling with conflicting emotions.

Part of me wants to run after Oliver's truck, to tell him that maybe, just maybe, I could see a future here in Benton Falls. But the larger part, the part that's protected me all these years, holds me back. Attachment leads to pain, it reminds me. Better to stay focused on my career, on the things I can control.

As I step inside, the warmth of the house envelops me like a hug. My eyes fall on the toy drive paperwork spread across the coffee table, and unbidden, an image of a child's face lighting up on Christmas morning flashes through my mind.

For a moment, I allow myself to imagine what it would be like to stay, to be part of this community, to build a life here with Oliver. The thought sends a pang through my chest, a mixture of longing and fear that leaves me breathless.

Shaking my head, I force the thoughts away. I'm a successful CEO. I don't need quaint small towns or charming department store owners or the warmth of community. I've built my life on hard work and independence, and I'm not about to throw that away for some holiday sentimentality.

But as I get ready for bed, I can't shake the feeling that something has shifted inside me. The armor I once wore to guard my heart now feels heavy, suffocating the very thing it was meant to protect.

Lying in bed, staring up at the ceiling, I hum "Silent Night," the memory of Oliver's hand brushing mine, sending a warmth through me that has nothing to do with my cozy blankets.

I fall asleep with the taste of peppermint cocoa on my lips and the echo of Christmas carols in my ears, my dreams filled with twinkling lights, children's laughter, and a pair of warm hazel eyes that seem to see right through to my soul.

In the morning, I wake to find a text from Oliver: "Thanks again for last night. Your help with the toy drive means more than you know. Coffee later to go over distribution plans?"

I stare at the message, my thumb hovering over the reply button. This is my chance to pull back, to reestablish the professional boundaries I've let slip. But I find myself typing: "Sounds great. Meet you at the cafe at 10?"

As I hit send, a small smile plays at my lips. Maybe, just maybe, I can allow myself to enjoy this Christmas in Benton Falls. After all, it's only temporary, right?

Eight

CHLOE

The bell above the door of Sweet Haven Bakery & Café jingles merrily as I step inside, a gust of cold air following me. The warm aroma of freshly baked cinnamon rolls and brewing coffee welcomes me, instantly thawing the chill from my bones. Christmas music plays softly in the background, and I hum along before I catch myself. What's happening to me?

I scan the cozy interior, taking in the rustic wooden beams overhead and the exposed brick walls adorned with vintage bakery signs. My gaze lands on Oliver, already seated at a corner table. He looks up and catches my eye, his face breaking into a warm smile that sends an unexpected flutter through my chest.

"Chloe." he calls out, waving me over. "I got you a latte. Hope that's okay."

As I make my way to the table, weaving between mismatched wooden chairs and tables, I'm struck by how at ease I feel. It's a far cry from the sleek, modern coffee shops I usually frequent in the city.

"Thanks," I say, sliding into the seat across from Oliver. I wrap my hands around the steaming mug, savoring its warmth. "That's perfect, actually."

Oliver beams at me, and I have to look away, suddenly flustered. What is wrong with me? I don't get flustered over small-town shop owners with kind eyes and charming smiles.

"So," I say, clearing my throat and pulling out my tablet. "I've been working on some ideas for the toy drive. I think if we implement a few key strategies, we could make this the most successful one yet."

Oliver leans forward, his eyes lighting up with interest. "I'm all ears. What have you got?"

For the next hour, we pour over spreadsheets and marketing plans. I explain my ideas for streamlining the donation process, implementing an online tracking system, and leveraging social media to reach a wider audience. Oliver listens intently, asking thoughtful questions and offering insights about the community that I hadn't considered.

As we talk, I can't help but notice the way the golden glow from the Edison bulb fixtures catches the flecks of green in Oliver's hazel eyes, or how his brow furrows adorably when he's concentrating. Stop it, Chloe, I scold myself. You're here to help with the toy drive, not to admire Oliver's... everything.

"This is incredible, Chloe," Oliver says, leaning back

in his chair with a look of awe. "I can't believe how much you've accomplished in such a short time. The kids of Benton Falls are going to have an amazing Christmas, thanks to you."

I feel a warmth spread through my chest at his words, and it has nothing to do with the latte I'm sipping. "It's not just me," I say, surprised by my modesty. "None of this would be possible without your connections in the community and your dedication to the cause."

Oliver reaches across the table and gives my hand a gentle squeeze. The touch sends a jolt of electricity up my arm, and for a moment, I forget to breathe.

"We make a good team," he says softly, his eyes meeting mine.

The intensity of his gaze is too much. I pull my hand away, focusing intently on my tablet screen. "Yes, well, there's still a lot to do," I say briskly, trying to ignore the hurt that flashes across Oliver's face.

Just then, a woman approaches our table. Her round face is flushed from the heat of the ovens, and flour dusts her curly auburn hair.

"How are you two doing?" she asks warmly. "Can I get you anything else? I just pulled a batch of my famous gingerbread cookies out of the oven."

"That sounds wonderful, Maggie," Oliver says. "We'll take a plate, please." He grins, then says, "Maggie, this is Chloe. She's helping me with the toy drive."

"Wonderful," Maggie smiles. "It's so nice to meet you."

I smile and nod. A second later, Maggie bustles away. I raise an eyebrow at Oliver. "Famous gingerbread cookies?"

He grins. "Oh, you're in for a treat. Maggie's gingerbread is legendary in Benton Falls. It's not really Christmas until you've had one of her cookies."

A few minutes later, Maggie returns with a plate piled high with gingerbread men, the scent of molasses and spices wafting through the air. "Here you go, dears," she says, setting the plate between us. "On the house. It's the least I can do for the dynamic duo behind this year's toy drive."

I start to protest, but Oliver cuts me off. "Thank you, Maggie. That's very kind of you."

As Maggie walks away, I take a bite of a gingerbread cookie, and my eyes widen in surprise. It's possibly the best thing I've ever tasted, the perfect balance of sweetness and spice melting on my tongue.

"Oh my goodness," I mumble around a mouthful of cookie. "These are incredible."

Oliver laughs, his eyes crinkling at the corners in a way that makes my heart do a little flip. "Told you. Maggie's cookies are magic."

As we continue to discuss the toy drive, munching on gingerbread, I find myself relaxing more and more. The cafe is bustling with activity, locals coming in and out, greeting each other warmly. More than once, someone stops by our table to chat with Oliver, and he introduces me with a proud, "This is Chloe, the brains behind our new toy drive system."

Each time, I'm met with genuine smiles and heartfelt thanks. It's... nice. Really nice, actually. For the first time in years, I feel like I'm part of something bigger than myself, something that matters beyond profit margins and market shares.

"You know," Oliver says, interrupting my thoughts, "I can't thank you enough for all your help with this, Chloe. It means more than you know."

I feel a blush creeping up my cheeks. "It's nothing, really. I'm just applying basic business principles to—"

"It's not nothing," Oliver interrupts gently. "You're making a real difference here. I just wish..."

He trails off, his expression suddenly clouding over. I lean forward, concerned. "You wish what?"

Oliver sighs, running a hand through his already tousled hair. "I wish I could apply some of your business savvy to the store. Things have been... tough lately."

My heart clenches at the worry in his eyes. "What do you mean? I thought the store was managing."

"If you mean getting by, then yes, although I'm not sure for how long," Oliver says. "We're still the heart of the community, especially during the holidays. But with the big box stores and online shopping... I'm worried about the future. About whether there will even be a Hanks' Department Store for the next generation."

The vulnerability in his voice tugs at something deep inside me. Before I can stop myself, I reach out and take his hand. "Oliver, I'm sure if we put our heads together, we can come up with some strategies to boost business."

This time, Oliver seems like he's open to my suggestions.

He looks up at me, hope shining in his eyes. "You'd do that? Help me with the store?"

I nod, squeezing his hand. "Of course. It's what I do."

For a moment, we just sit there, hands clasped, eyes locked. The hustle and bustle of the cafe fades away, and all I can see is Oliver. The warmth of his touch, the gratitude in his gaze, the way his thumb is gently stroking the back of my hand... it's all too much and not enough at the same time.

Suddenly, reality comes crashing back in. What am I doing? I'm leaving Benton Falls after the holidays. I can't let myself get attached, can't let myself care this much. I pull my hand away abruptly, clearing my throat.

"So, um, what ideas did you have for the store?" I ask, my voice sounding strained even to my own ears.

Oliver blinks, looking a bit dazed. "Oh, right. Well, I was thinking maybe we could expand our online presence? Set up an e-commerce site?"

I nod, slipping back into business mode. "That's a good start. We could also look at your inventory management, maybe streamline your supply chain..."

As we dive into discussing the store's business model, I can feel a tension building between us. Our approaches are fundamentally different—I'm all about efficiency and modernization, while Oliver is focused on preserving the store's heritage and personal touch.

"But Chloe," Oliver says, frustration creeping into

his voice, "if we automate everything and cut back on staff, we'll lose the personal connections that make Hanks' special. Our customers come to us because they know they'll be greeted by name, because we remember their kids' sizes and their grandma's favorite perfume."

I sigh, exasperated. "I understand that, Oliver, but you can't run a business on sentiment alone. You need to adapt to survive in today's market."

"At what cost, though?" Oliver counters. "If we lose our soul, what's the point of surviving?"

We stare at each other across the table, the gulf between our worldviews suddenly seeming impossibly wide. How could I have thought, even for a moment, that this could work? That I could fit into Oliver's world, or he into mine?

The silence stretches between us, thick with unspoken words and missed connections. Finally, I stand up, gathering my things.

"I should go," I say, not meeting Oliver's eyes. "I have some work to catch up on."

Oliver nods, his expression unreadable. "Of course. Thanks for your help with the toy drive, Chloe. I really appreciate it."

As I walk out of the cafe, the cheerful jingle of the bell seems to mock me. The cold air hits me like a slap, and I welcome it, using it to clear my head of the confused jumble of emotions swirling inside me.

What was I thinking, letting myself get so invested in this town, in Oliver? This isn't my world. I don't belong here, with its quaint traditions and its emphasis on community over profit.

And yet... as I walk back to my grandmother's house, I can't shake the feeling that I'm leaving something important behind in that warm, cozy cafe. The memory of Oliver's hand in mine, of the hope in his eyes when I offered to help, of the way he lights up when talking about his store and his community—it all tugs at something deep inside me, something I thought I'd buried long ago.

Back at the house, I throw myself into work my company says I'm not to worry about, determined to push aside these confusing feelings. But as I stare at spreadsheets and profit projections, my mind keeps wandering back to the toy drive, to the joy on the faces of the people I've met in Benton Falls, to Oliver's warm smile.

For the first time in years, I question everything I thought I knew about success and happiness. Is my life in the city, with its relentless pursuit of the next big deal, really all there is? Or is there something to be said for the kind of success Oliver values - the success measured in lives touched and community strengthened?

As night falls, I stand at the window, looking out at the twinkling Christmas lights of Benton Falls. The town seems to glow with a warmth that has nothing to do with electricity, a warmth that comes from the connections between people, from traditions passed down through generations, from the simple joy of giving.

I think about the toy drive, about the children who

will wake up on Christmas morning to find gifts under their tree. I think about Oliver, working tirelessly to keep his family's legacy alive while still finding time to organize charity events and greet every customer by name.

With a sigh, I sink onto the couch, burying my face in my hands. I don't know what to do, how to reconcile these conflicting parts of myself. The driven business-woman and the girl who's starting to remember what it feels like to care, to belong.

As I sit there, the scent of gingerbread still clinging to my clothes, I realize that I have a choice to make, and I don't know what the right answer is.

The toy drive spreadsheets still open on my laptop seem to mock me from across the room. They represent everything I thought I wanted—efficiency, success, control. But now, they also remind me of Oliver's warm laugh, of the gratitude in people's eyes when they thank me for my help, of the feeling of being part of something bigger than myself.

Closing my eyes, I let the quiet of the house wash over me. In the distance, I can hear the faint sound of Christmas carols drifting from a neighbor's house. It's a reminder of the world outside, a world full of warmth and connection and, yes, complications.

I drift off to sleep right there on the couch, as one thought circles in my mind: What if the most successful thing I could do, the bravest thing, would be to open my heart to the magic of Benton Falls? To Oliver? To a different life than the one I've always imagined for myself?

It's a terrifying thought. But as I slip into dreams filled with the jingling of sleigh bells and the warmth of Oliver's smile, I can't help but wonder if maybe, just maybe, it might also be the most rewarding.

Nine

S aturday morning, I'm loitering outside Sweet Haven Bakery & Café, like some kind of stalker person. My breath puffs out in little clouds as I press my nose against the frosty window. Inside, Chloe and Oliver are huddled over a table, looking all cozy and cute, which feels promising.

I watch as Oliver says something that makes Chloe laugh. Her face lights up, and for a second, I think this might be it. My ticket to full angelhood, baby. But then, because the universe hates me, Chloe pulls away when Oliver tries to touch her hand. Seriously? I've seen glaciers move faster than these two.

"For the love, Chloe," I mutter, "stop being so stubborn."

A couple walking by gives me a weird look. Right, talking to myself in public. Smooth move, Rebecca. I flash them my best 'I'm totally normal' smile and pretend to be super interested in the cafe's Christmas lights.

Inside, Chloe's gathering her stuff like the cafe's on fire. Oliver looks like someone just told him Christmas is canceled. As Chloe hustles out the door, I have to resist the urge to trip her. Not that I would. Probably.

I trail after her, trying to blend in with the crowd. It's times like these I wish I had invisibility powers. Being a guardian angel in training sucks sometimes.

As I walk, I find myself ranting at the sky. "Seriously, what's a girl gotta do to get through to her? I'm trying my best here." A squirrel pauses its nut-gathering to give me a 'you crazy' look. Thanks to my animal-speaking powers, I hear its thoughts loud and clear.

"You humans are weird," it chitters. "Why not just eat nuts and chill?"

I snort. "Trust me, fur ball, I wish it was that simple. But no, humans have to make everything complicated. It's exhausting."

The squirrel twitches its tail in what I'm pretty sure is the rodent equivalent of an eye-roll before scampering off. Rude.

I spend the rest of Saturday trailing Chloe around town, watching her throw herself into work on the toy drive. She's got spreadsheets for her spreadsheets, I swear. But now and then, I catch her staring off into space with this lost look on her face. Progress, maybe?

Sunday morning rolls around, and I'm back on Chloe-watch. The church on Oak Street fits right into this Christmas-crazed town, all red brick and white trim against the snowy backdrop. I slip inside just as the service is starting; the warmth hitting me like a wall. The smell of wood polish and candles fills the air, and for a second, I'm hit with a pang of homesickness for the celestial realm. Weird.

I spot Chloe sitting near the back, looking like she'd rather be anywhere else. But as the service goes on, I notice her relax as the choir sings "O Holy Night," I swear I see her eyes get misty.

After the service, there's a pageant rehearsal. Chloe tries to make a break for it, but gets roped into helping by a harried-looking mom with an armful of angel wings. I stifle a laugh as Chloe awkwardly tries to attach a pair of glittery wings to a squirming five-year-old.

"Hold still, sweetie," Chloe says, her voice gentler than I've ever heard it. "We want to make sure you're the prettiest angel in the pageant, right?"

The little girl beams up at her, and I feel a weird twinge in my chest. Is this what progress feels like?

Just then, Oliver walks in, his arms full of more costume pieces. The tension between him and Chloe hits like a heavenly thunderbolt. But then some kid trips, sending tinsel flying everywhere, and they both rush to help. Their hands touch, and for a second, I think this might be it. But nope, Chloe pulls away faster than Lucifer fell from heaven.

I slump in my seat, groaning internally. This is harder than I thought it would be. Why can't Chloe just get with the program already?

As the rehearsal goes on, I keep my eyes glued to Chloe. She's trying so hard to keep up her ice queen act, but I can see it slipping. When she helps a kid with his lines, her smile is genuine. When the kids sing "Away in a Manger," her eyes get all misty again. It's like watching a glacier melt, painfully slow but definitely happening.

When Chloe sneaks out the side door after rehearsal, I follow her. Time to work some angelic magic.

"Oh." she jumps when she sees me. "Rebecca. Where did you come from?"

I paste on my best 'just a normal human' smile. "Oh, you know, I was just... around. The rehearsal's looking great, huh?"

Chloe nods, but her smile's about as real as my human disguise. We step outside, and I notice her shiver. Without thinking, I unwrap my scarf and hold it out to her. "Here. You look like you're freezing your designer boots off."

She hesitates, then takes it. As she wraps it around her neck, I can practically see some of her walls coming down.

"Thanks," she says softly. Then, "Rebecca, can I ask you something?"

"Shoot," I say, trying not to sound too eager. Is this it? Is she finally opening up?

Chloe fidgets with the scarf. "Do you ever feel like... like you don't belong somewhere, even when everyone says you do?"

Oh boy, do I ever. Try being the only angel more interested in Earth's stock market than harp lessons. But I can't say that, so instead I go for, "All the time. But here's the thing - sometimes the place where you feel most out of place is exactly where you're supposed to be. It's where you grow the most, you know?"

Since when did I start speaking "Henry"?

Chloe looks at me like I've grown a second head. "That's... surprisingly deep, Rebecca."

I shrug, trying to play it cool even though inside I'm doing a victory dance. "I have my moments. Hey, want to grab a coffee? I hear Maggie's peppermint mochas are killer."

For a second, I think she's going to bail. But then she nods, a tiny smile appearing. "You know what? That sounds nice."

As we crunch through the snow towards the café, I send up a little prayer of thanks. It's not much, but it's progress. And right now, I'll take what I can get.

Later that night, as I'm getting ready to head back to the celestial realm, I can't help but feel... different. I've learned a lot about Chloe today, sure, but I've also learned something about myself. Maybe being a guardian angel isn't about grand gestures or miraculous interventions. Maybe it's about being there, offering a scarf or a friendly ear when it's needed most.

As I feel the tingle of celestial energy whisking me away, I take one last look at Benton Falls, all lit up for Christmas. "Don't screw this up, Chloe," I mutter. "Some of us have wings riding on this, you know."

The heavenly realm materializes around me, all shimmery and perfect as always. I decide it won't hurt to check in with Henry and head down the pearly path towards Henry's office, trying to ignore the curious looks from other angels. Yeah, yeah, the weather girl's heading to the big boss's office. Take a picture, it'll last longer.

Just as I'm about to enter the building, I hear a voice that makes me want to teleport right back to Earth.

"Well, well, if it isn't our little earthbound forecaster," Gina says, landing in front of me with annoying grace. "How's the weather down there? Still cloudy with a chance of failure?"

I plaster on a smile so fake it would make a pageant queen proud. "Actually, Gina, things are going great. But thanks for caring. Really. It warms my heart."

Gina looks like she's just bitten into a lemon. Before she can come up with another zinger, Henry appears along the path.

"Rebecca," he says, eyes twinkling like he knows exactly what he's saving me from. "Just the angel I was looking for."

I smile and meet up with Henry, but not before shooting Gina a smug look. Take that, Miss Perfect Wings.

"Shall we take a walk?" Henry says, setting an easy pace. "Tell me all about your adventures with Chloe."

For the next hour, I spill everything - Chloe's baby steps with the toy drive, her hot-and-cold thing with Oliver, and the Great Café Disaster of this afternoon.

When I finish, Henry strokes his beard, looking thoughtful. "You've made some good progress, Rebecca," he says. "But something's bothering you, isn't it?"

I sigh dramatically, slumping further into the chair. "It's just... I thought I had it all figured out, you know?

Get Chloe to fall for Oliver, cue the Christmas spirit, boom - wings for Rebecca. But now... I don't know. What if I'm making things worse? What if Oliver isn't the key to all this?"

Henry chuckles, the sound reminding me of jingle bells. "Oh, Rebecca, always so focused on the endgame. But tell me, what have you learned from your time on Earth?"

I scrunch up my face, thinking hard. "Well... humans are way more complicated than they need to be. You can't force someone to open up - they've gotta do it themselves. And sometimes, little things matter more than big, showy gestures."

Henry beams at me like I've just discovered gravity or something. "Exactly. And how can you use those lessons with Chloe?"

I chew on my lip, considering. "I guess... I need to stop trying to force things. Give Chloe chances to open up, but let her choose to do it. And maybe focus more on the small stuff instead of trying to create some big, romantic movie moment."

"Precisely," Henry says, looking prouder than I've ever seen him. "Remember, Rebecca, your job isn't to play matchmaker—leave that to the cupids. It's to help Chloe rediscover the spirit of giving, of family, of Christmas. That can happen in many ways."

I nod slowly, feeling like a weight's been lifted off my shoulders. "You're right. I've been focusing on the whole Chloe-and-Oliver thing that I've been missing other ways to help her connect with people."

Henry stands up, stretching. "Excellent. Now, I believe you have a weather forecast to deliver?"

I groan, but there's no real annoyance behind it. "Do I have to? It's not like anyone's going to keel over in shock if I predict another perfect day."

Henry's eyes twinkle mischievously. "Oh, I don't know about that. I hear there might be a slight chance of celestial snowflakes tomorrow. Just to shake things up a bit."

I laugh, surprised to find that I'm actually kind of excited about my weather gig for once. "Celestial snowflakes, huh? Now that could be fun."

After I say goodbye to Henry, I head to the Weather Forecasting Department. My mind's buzzing with ideas. Maybe I'll use my time powers to do a slo-mo snowfall demo, or use my gift of tongues to deliver the forecast in every language ever.

The other angels look up in shock as I burst through the door, grinning like a maniac. "Who's ready for some heavenly precipitation?" I announce, clapping my hands together.

As I step up to the celestial weather map, I can feel the change in the air. Maybe, just maybe, I'm getting the hang of this guardian angel gig after all.

Wings, here I come.

Ten

CHLOE

The scent of fresh ink and new paper fills my nose as I step into the Benton Falls Elementary School gymnasium. It's been transformed into a winter wonderland of books, with rows upon rows of tables stacked high with colorful titles. Twinkling lights strung across the ceiling cast a warm, festive glow over everything, and garlands of holly and evergreens wrap around the windows and doorways. It's like walking into a Christmas card come to life.

I adjust the strap of my designer handbag, feeling distinctly out of place among the excited children darting between tables in their cozy sweaters and Santa hats. What am I doing here? I should be back at the house, working on year-end reports and strategizing for the next quarter—my idea of a vacation.

But then I catch sight of Rebecca, waving enthusiastically from behind a table piled high with picture books. Her golden hair is tied back with a red ribbon, and she's wearing a festive sweater that would look ridiculous on anyone else but somehow works on her.

"Chloe. You made it," she calls out, her voice carrying over the soft Christmas music playing in the background, as though she left me any choice when she showed up at my house bright and early this morning. Rebecca insisted "the book fair is short on volunteers", and "we can't do that to the kids". I think she must have a master's degree in Artful Persuasion. "Come on, we need help at the checkout table."

I sigh, resigning myself to an afternoon of... what exactly? Selling books to children? It seems so far removed from my usual world of boardrooms and business deals. But I did promise I'd help, and if there's one thing Chloe Anderson doesn't do, it's break promises.

As I make my way to the checkout table, I'm struck by the warmth and joy radiating from everyone around me. Parents chat animatedly with teachers, sipping hot cocoa from paper cups. A group of kids huddle around a display of fantasy novels, their eyes wide with excitement as they debate which dragon story looks the coolest.

"Here," Rebecca says, thrusting a Santa hat into my hands as I reach the table. "Put this on. It's part of the uniform."

I eye the hat skeptically. "I don't do hats. They mess up my hair."

Rebecca rolls her eyes good-naturedly. "Come on, Chloe. It's for the kids. Get into the spirit."

With a reluctant grumble, I put on the hat. It feels silly and childish, but when I catch sight of my reflection in a nearby window, I'm surprised to find that I don't hate it as much as I thought I would.

The next few hours pass in a blur of transactions, gift-wrapping, and more interaction with children than I've had in years. At first, it's overwhelming. I'm used to dealing with CEOs and investors, not seven-year-olds arguing over whether to buy the book about unicorns or the one about space pirates.

But as the afternoon wears on, I find myself... enjoying it? There's something infectious about the kids' enthusiasm, their unabashed excitement over stories and adventures. When a little girl with pigtails and missing front teeth tells me earnestly that she's buying a book to read to her little brother who's in the hospital, I feel a lump form in my throat.

"That's very kind of you," I tell her, carefully wrapping the book in shiny paper. "I'm sure your brother will love it."

The girl beams at me, and for a moment, I'm transported back to my childhood. I remember the joy of losing myself in a good book, of escaping the harsh realities of foster homes and never quite belonging. Books were my refuge then, my ticket to worlds where anything was possible.

As I hand the wrapped book to the little girl, I make a split-second decision. "Wait," I say, reaching for my wallet. "Pick out another book. On me. One for you this time."

The girl's eyes widen in disbelief. "Really? Are you sure?"

I nod, feeling a warmth spread through my chest that has nothing to do with the overheated gymnasium. "Absolutely. Everyone deserves a little magic of their own."

As the girl scampers off to choose another book, I catch Rebecca watching me with a knowing smile. "What?" I ask, feeling oddly defensive.

She just shakes her head, still smiling. "Nothing. It's just nice to see you getting into the spirit of things."

I'm about to argue that I'm not getting into any spirit, thank you very much, when Oliver appears at the table, his arms laden with more books.

"Hey, Chloe," he says, his smile doing funny things to my insides. "Rebecca roped you into volunteering too, huh?"

I nod, suddenly very aware of the ridiculous Santa hat perched on my head. "Apparently, I'm a sucker for a good cause."

Oliver's eyes crinkle at the corners as he laughs. "Well, it suits you. The hat, I mean. And the volunteering."

For a moment, we just stand there, smiling at each other like idiots. Then a small voice pipes up, "Excuse me, can I buy this book, please?"

We both jump, startled out of our little bubble. As I ring up the purchase, I can feel Oliver's eyes on me, and I have to resist the urge to smooth my hair or check my lipstick.

The rest of the afternoon flies by in a whirlwind of transactions, laughter, and more warm looks from Oliver than I care to admit. By the time the last customer leaves and we pack up, I'm exhausted but filled with a sense of accomplishment I haven't felt in a long time.

"Great job today, everyone," the principal announces, beaming at all of us. "Thanks to your hard work, we've raised enough money to buy new books for every classroom and donate a bunch to the children's hospital."

A cheer goes up from the volunteers, and I join in, caught up in the collective joy of a job well done.

As we file out of the school, the frosty night air hits me like a shock after the warmth of the gymnasium. Snowflakes dance in the glow of the streetlights, and the sound of distant carolers drifts on the wind.

"So," Oliver says, falling into step beside me. "Any plans for tomorrow night?"

I shake my head. "Not really. Why?"

"Well, there's caroling in the town square. I thought maybe... if you're not busy..." He trails off, looking uncharacteristically nervous.

Singing again? I should say no. I have work to do, emails to send, a life waiting for me back in the city. But looking at Oliver's hopeful face, dusted with snowflakes and lit by the warm glow of Christmas lights, I say, "Sure, that sounds nice."

His answering smile is brighter than all the Christmas lights in Benton Falls combined.

The next evening finds me standing in the town square, surrounded by what seems like the entire population of Benton Falls. The majestic courthouse clock tower looms above us, its face illuminated and hands pointing to just a few minutes before seven.

I shift from foot to foot, grateful for the warm boots Rebecca insisted I borrow. My designer heels might look great, but they're not exactly made for standing around in the snow.

"Here," Oliver says, appearing at my elbow and handing me a steaming cup. "Hot chocolate. Maggie's secret recipe."

I take a sip, and my eyes widen in surprise. It's rich and creamy, with just a hint of peppermint. "This is delicious," I admit.

Oliver grins. "Told you. Maggie's hot chocolate is legendary around here."

As the clock strikes seven, a hush falls over the crowd. Then, from somewhere near the front, a voice sings "Silent Night." Slowly, others join in, the melody swelling until it seems like the whole town is singing in harmony.

I don't know the words, so I just stand there, sipping my hot chocolate and listening. It's beautiful in a way I can't quite describe—not perfect like a professional choir, but real and raw and full of heart.

As the carol ends and another begins, I feel Oliver's hand slip into mine. I should pull away. I should maintain my distance, remember that this isn't my world, that I'm leaving after the holidays. But his hand is warm and strong, and in that moment, I can't bring myself to let go.

We stand like that through "Deck the Halls" and "Jingle Bells" and half a dozen other carols I vaguely remember from childhood. I don't sing, but I sway slightly to the music, caught up in the magic of the moment.

As the final notes of "We Wish You a Merry Christmas" fade away, replaced by the cheerful chatter of the dispersing crowd, Oliver turns to me. In the glow of the Christmas lights, his eyes seem to shine with something more than just a reflection.

"Chloe," he says softly, "I—"

But whatever he was about to say is cut off by a commotion near the courthouse steps. We turn to see a group of people gathering around someone who seems to have slipped on a patch of ice.

Without hesitation, Oliver rushes over to help, pulling me along with him. As we get closer, Oliver sighs, "It's Mr. Jenkins, the Postman."

"Are you alright, Bill?" Oliver asks, helping the older man to his feet.

Mr. Jenkins winces as he puts weight on his right ankle. "I think I might have twisted it," he says. "Darn ice."

"Let's get you inside where it's warm," Oliver says. "We can call the doctor from there if needed."

As Oliver helps Mr. Jenkins limp towards the courthouse, which is still open for the caroling event, I follow along, unsure of what to do but unable to just walk away.

Inside, Oliver settles Mr. Jenkins into a chair while someone goes to call the doctor. I hover awkwardly nearby, feeling useless.

"Is there anything I can do?" I ask.

Oliver looks up at me, a grateful smile on his face. "Actually, yeah. Could you run over to the store and grab the first aid kit? It's behind the counter."

I nod, relieved to have a task. "Of course. I'll be right back."

The cold air hits me like a slap as I step outside, but I barely notice it as I hurry towards Hanks' Department Store. The streets are mostly empty now, everyone having dispersed after the caroling, and my footsteps echo in the quiet night.

As I unlock the store—Oliver had given me a key for the toy drive inventory—the familiar bell jingles above the door. In the dim light filtering in from the street, the store looks different—shadowy and mysterious, full of potential.

I find the first aid kit easily enough, but as I'm about to leave, something catches my eye. It's a ledger, left open on the counter. I know I shouldn't look, that it's none of my business, but a lifetime of business instincts are hard to ignore.

What I see makes my heart sink. The numbers are worse than I thought. Much worse. At this rate, Hanks' Department Store won't make it past the new year.

I stand there for a long moment, the first aid kit forgotten in my hands, as a plan begins to form in my mind. It's crazy. It's impulsive. It goes against every practical business decision I've ever made.

But as I think about Oliver—his kindness, his dedication to this town, the way he lights up when he talks about the store's history—I know I have to do something.

Back at the courthouse, the doctor has arrived and is examining Mr. Jenkins' ankle. Oliver takes the first aid kit from me with a grateful smile, and I try to act normal, like I haven't just made a decision that could change everything.

Later that night, after we've seen Mr. Jenkins safely home and said our goodnights, I sit at the desk in my grandmother's house, staring at my laptop screen. The glow of the Christmas lights outside filters through the window, casting colorful shadows across the keyboard.

With a deep breath, I type out an email to my financial advisor. The plan is simple but risky—liquidate some of my personal investments and use the money to anonymously invest in Hanks' Department Store. Enough to keep it afloat, to give Oliver a fighting chance.

As I hit send, a mix of emotions washes over me. Fear, excitement, doubt. This must be Christmas madness. But underneath it all, there's a warm feeling I can't quite name. Is this what it feels like to truly give? To put someone else's needs before your own?

I close my laptop and walk to the window, looking out at the snow-covered streets of Benton Falls. The town is quiet now, most windows dark except for the glow of Christmas lights. But in my mind's eye, I can see it bustling with life—families shopping at Hanks', children pressing their noses against the display windows, Oliver's face lit up with joy as he helps a customer find the perfect gift.

For the first time since I arrived in Benton Falls, I allow myself to imagine a future here. Not just for the holidays, but beyond. A future where I'm part of this community, where my skills and resources are used not just for profit, but for the good of others.

It's a terrifying thought. But as I crawl into bed, the memory of Oliver's hand in mine still tingling on my skin. It's also strangely exhilarating.

Tomorrow, I decide as I drift off to sleep, I'll tell Oliver about my idea for modernizing the store's inventory system. Not as a CEO offering unsolicited advice, but as a friend who wants to help. And maybe, just maybe, as something more.

The last thing I see before sleep claims me is the gentle fall of snow outside my window. Each flake a tiny miracle of possibility. And for the first time in years, I fall asleep with a smile on my face, my heart full of the spirit of giving that seems to permeate every corner of Benton Falls.

Eleven

CHLOE

I make my way through the bustling Christmas market in the Benton Falls city park. Twinkling lights strung between wooden stalls cast a warm glow over everything, transforming the familiar space into a winter wonderland. Spice and pine mingle with the aroma of roasting chestnuts, creating an intoxicating blend that seems to embody the very essence of the holiday season.

I pause at a stall selling hand-knitted scarves, running my fingers over the soft wool. A week ago, I would have scoffed at the idea of wearing anything not bearing a designer label. Now, I seriously consider buying one. What is happening to me?

"Chloe. Over here."

I turn to see Oliver waving at me from near the ice skating rink. His wide smile is punctuated by his bright hazel eyes as his gaze meets mine. He's bundled up in a forest green parka, a matching knit hat pulled low over his ears. The sight of him sends a flutter through my stomach that has nothing to do with the cold.

As I make my way over, weaving between families and couples enjoying the festive atmosphere, I can't help but feel a sense of giddy anticipation. The knowledge of what I've done—the anonymous donation to save Oliver's store—sits warm in my chest, a delicious secret that makes me want to laugh out loud.

"Hey," I say as I reach him, suddenly feeling shy. "Nice hat."

Oliver grins, his cheeks rosy from the cold. "Thanks. My mom made it for me. Ready to show off your skating skills?"

I glance at the rink, where people of all ages are gliding—or in some cases, stumbling—across the ice. "I should warn you, I haven't been skating since I was a kid. I might be a bit rusty."

"Don't worry," Oliver says, his eyes twinkling. "I'll catch you if you fall."

The words send a warmth spreading through me that has nothing to do with my thick coat. As we make our way to the rental booth to get our skates, I find myself hyper-aware of Oliver's presence beside me—the brush of his arm against mine, the sound of his laughter as he jokes with the attendant.

"Here," he says, handing me a pair of white skates. "Let's sit over there to put them on."

We make our way to a bench near the rink. As I lace up my skates, I can't help but notice how at ease Oliver seems, greeting everyone who passes by with a warm smile or a friendly word. It's so different from the corporate world I'm used to, where interactions are often calculated and relationships are measured by their potential value.

"All set?" Oliver asks, standing up and offering me his hand.

I nod, suddenly nervous. What if I fall flat on my face in front of everyone? But as I take Oliver's hand and he helps me to my feet, I'm struck by how solid and warm his grip is. For a moment, I forget to be worried about falling.

We make our way to the rink's entrance, the sound of blades scraping against ice and cheerful laughter growing louder. As we step onto the ice, I wobble slightly, my legs feeling unsteady.

"Whoa there," Oliver says, his arm immediately going around my waist to steady me. "I've got you. Just take it slow."

The feel of his arm around me sends a jolt through my system that has nothing to do with the cold or my unsteady balance. I nod, not trusting myself to speak, and we glide forward slowly.

At first, I'm tense, too focused on not falling to enjoy the experience. But as we make our way around the rink, Oliver's steady presence beside me, I begin to relax. The rhythm of gliding across the ice comes back to me, muscle memory from childhood winters spent at the local rink in my hometown.

"See? You're a natural," Oliver says, his voice warm with encouragement.

I laugh, the sound surprising me with its lightness. "I wouldn't go that far. But it is fun."

As we continue to skate, I take in the surrounding scene. Children zoom past, their laughter ringing out in the crisp air. Couples hold hands as they glide along, lost in their own little worlds. The twinkling lights reflect off the ice, creating a magical, shimmering effect.

"Oh, look," Oliver says, nodding towards a corner of the rink. "They've set up a photo booth. Want to get a picture?"

I hesitate for a moment. A photo would be evidence of this night, of my time in Benton Falls. Something tangible to remind me of... what? This town that isn't mine, this life that isn't real?

But then I look at Oliver's hopeful face, and I nod. "Sure, why not?"

We make our way off the ice and over to the booth. It's decorated to look like a giant snow globe, complete with fake snow and twinkling lights. As we squeeze into the small space together, I'm acutely aware of how close Oliver is, the warmth of his body next to mine.

"Okay, ready?" he says, pressing the button to start the countdown. "Say cheese."

The flash goes off four times in quick succession. As we step out of the booth, the strip of photos prints out. Oliver takes it, grinning as he looks at the results.

"Oh, these are great," he says, showing me.

I lean in to look, and my breath catches in my throat. The first photo shows us both smiling at the camera—nothing unusual. But in the second, Oliver is looking at me instead of the camera, his expression soft. In the third, I'm laughing at something he said, my head thrown back in a way I barely recognize as myself. And in the fourth...

In the fourth photo, we're looking at each other, and the connection between us is almost palpable. I look happier than I've seen myself in years.

"We should get back to skating," I say quickly, feeling suddenly overwhelmed. "I think I'm ready to try it on my own now."

Oliver nods, tucking the photo strip into his pocket. "Lead the way."

Back on the ice, I push off with newfound confidence. The cold air whips past my face as I pick up speed, and I feel a rush of exhilaration. I can't remember the last time I felt so... free.

I complete a lap around the rink and find Oliver waiting for me, a proud smile on his face. "Look at you go," he says. "I knew you had it in you."

As I come to a stop beside him, I'm filled with a sudden, overwhelming urge to kiss him. The thought shocks me so much that I lose my balance, stumbling forward.

Oliver catches me, his brawny arms wrapping around me. For a moment, we're frozen like that, our faces inches apart. I can see the flecks of gold in his hazel eyes, feel the warmth of his breath on my cheek.

"Thanks," I whisper, my heart pounding.

"Anytime," he says softly.

We stay like that for a beat too long before slowly

separating. As we resume skating, side by side now, I can feel something has shifted between us. The air seems charged with possibility.

After a while, we decide to take a break and explore the Christmas market. Oliver buys us both cups of hot cocoa, and the rich, chocolaty scent wafts up, warming my cold nose.

"So," Oliver says as we wander among the stalls, "how are you liking Benton Falls' Christmas traditions so far?"

I take a sip of my cocoa, considering. "It's... different from what I'm used to," I admit. "But in a good way. Everything feels so... genuine."

Oliver nods, understanding in his eyes. "That's what I love about this town. Everyone really comes together, especially during the holidays."

As we walk, I open up to Oliver in a way I never have before. I tell him about my childhood, about the Christmases spent in foster homes where I never quite felt like I belonged. About how I threw myself into my career, thinking success and money would fill the void I felt inside.

Oliver listens attentively, his hand finding mine as we walk. The warmth of his touch seems to travel up my arm, thawing something frozen inside me.

"You know," he says softly, "it's never too late to create new traditions. To find a place where you belong."

His words hit me like a gentle wave, washing away some of the walls I've built around myself. For the first time, I allow myself to imagine what it would be like to stay in Benton Falls, to be part of this community. To be with Oliver.

The thought should terrify me. A week ago, it would have. But now, as we stand in the glow of the Christmas lights, surrounded by the warmth and joy of the season, it fills me with a sense of peace instead.

We make our way to the reindeer petting zoo, where children are squealing with delight as they feed carrots to the gentle creatures. Oliver immediately starts chatting with the caretaker, asking about the reindeer's diet and care routine.

As I watch him interact with the animals and the people around us, I'm struck by how effortlessly he connects with everyone. It's a skill I've always admired in others, but never quite mastered myself.

"Want to try it?" Oliver asks, holding out a carrot to me.

I hesitate, eyeing the large animal warily. "I don't know..."

"Come on," he encourages. "Donner here is a real sweetheart. Aren't you, buddy?"

The reindeer snorts softly, as if in agreement. With a deep breath, I take the carrot from Oliver and hold it out. Donner's velvety nose brushes against my palm as he gently takes the treat, and I can't help but laugh at the ticklish sensation.

"See? Not so scary after all," Oliver says, his hand resting lightly on the small of my back.

As we continue to explore the market, I find myself relaxing more and more. We sample local cheeses, admire handcrafted ornaments, and even try our hand at decorating gingerbread cookies at a workshop set up in one stall.

My cookie ends up looking like a disaster, with icing smeared everywhere and candies placed haphazardly. Oliver's is a work of art, with delicate piping and a perfect candy cane border.

"How are you so good at this?" I ask, laughing as I compare our creations.

Oliver shrugs, a mischievous glint in his eye. "Years of practice. You should see the gingerbread houses we make at the store every year."

As the evening wears on, the market becomes even more magical. The lights seem to twinkle brighter against the darkening sky, and the sound of carolers fills the air. Oliver and I find ourselves drawn back to the skating rink, now illuminated by strings of fairy lights.

This time, as we glide across the ice hand in hand, I feel completely at ease. The fear of falling, both literally and figuratively, seems to have melted away. Instead, I'm filled with a warmth that has nothing to do with my winter coat and everything to do with the man beside me.

"Chloe," Oliver says softly as we come to a stop at the edge of the rink. "I'm really glad you're here."

The sincerity in his voice makes my heart skip a beat. "Me too," I reply, surprised by how much I mean it.

For a moment, we just stand there, our hands intertwined, gazing at each other. The world seems to fade away, the bustling market becoming a quiet backdrop to this perfect moment. Oliver's hazel eyes, flecked with gold in the soft light of the lamps, hold mine. I can see every emotion I'm feeling reflected back at me—hope, joy, and a touch of nervous excitement.

Then, slowly, Oliver leans in. I meet him halfway, my heart racing in anticipation. As our lips come together in a tender kiss, I'm overwhelmed by a rush of sensations. His lips are soft and warm against mine, a stark contrast to the chilly winter air around us. The kiss tastes like hot cocoa and possibility, sweet and comforting, yet thrilling with the promise of new beginnings.

I catch the faint scent of his cologne mingling with the crisp winter air and a hint of sweet vanilla from the nearby food truck. The gentle pressure of his lips sends a tingling sensation through my body, from the top of my head to the tips of my toes.

As we kiss, I hear the town clock chime the hour. The deep, resonant tones seem to reverberate through me, marking not just the time, but the start of a new chapter in my life. The sound mingles with the soft rustle of snowflakes falling around us and the distant echoes of Christmas shoppers.

Oliver's arms encircle me, strong and secure. I feel the rough wool of his coat beneath my fingertips as I rest my hands on his chest, the steady beat of his heart a comforting rhythm against my palm. The warmth of his embrace contrasts deliciously with the cold snowflakes melting on my cheeks.

When we finally part, both a little breathless, I open my eyes to see Oliver's face lit up with a joy that I'm sure mirrors my own. His smile is soft and tender, filled with a warmth that makes me feel cherished and cared for.

"Wow," he whispers, his breath forming a small cloud in the cold air between us.

I can't help but laugh softly, feeling giddy and light-hearted. "Wow indeed," I agree, my voice barely above a whisper.

As we stand there, still wrapped in each other's arms, the world slowly comes back into focus around us. The twinkling lights, the gently falling snow, the bustling Christmas market - it all seems brighter, more vivid than before. This kiss, this moment, has awakened all my senses, making me feel more alive than I've ever felt.

It's as if I'm experiencing the magic of Christmas, of love, of Benton Falls, all at once, with every fiber of my being. And as Oliver takes my hand, ready to continue our evening stroll, I know with absolute certainty that this is just the beginning of something wonderful.

As we make our way off the ice, I'm struck by how different I feel from the woman who arrived in Benton Falls just a couple of weeks ago. The drive for success and financial security that has defined me for so long seems less important now. Instead, I find myself valuing the connections I've made, the joy I've found in simple moments like this.

We return our skates and begin the walk back to town, our hands still linked. The streets are quiet now, most of the townspeople having headed home for the night. But the Christmas lights still twinkle merrily, and the occasional sound of laughter drifts from houses we pass.

"So," Oliver says as we near my grandmother's house. "What did you think of your first Benton Falls Community Ice Skating Night?"

I pretend to consider for a moment. "Well, the company was pretty good," I tease. "But I think I might need a few more lessons before I'm ready for the Olympics."

Oliver laughs, pulling me closer. "I'd be happy to volunteer as your personal instructor."

As we reach my front porch, I find myself reluctant to say goodnight. The evening has been like something out of a dream, and I'm afraid that once it ends, the spell will be broken.

"Oliver," I say, turning to face him. "I want you to know... I'm really happy I came to Benton Falls. And I'm really happy I met you."

The smile he gives me in response is so warm, so full of genuine affection, that it takes my breath away. "I'm happy too, Chloe. Happier than I've been in a long time."

He leans in for another kiss, this one deeper and more passionate than the first, like he's trying to tell me something, our hearts whispering to one another. When we finally pull apart, we're both a little breathless.

"Goodnight, Chloe," Oliver says softly, his forehead resting against mine.

"Goodnight, Oliver," I reply.

As I watch him walk away, his figure fading into the

snowy night, I'm filled with a sense of contentment I've never experienced before. The old Chloe would panic right now, making plans to leave town and forget this ever happened. But as I unlock my door and step inside, I realize I don't want to run anymore.

For the first time in a long time, I feel like I might belong. And as I get ready for bed, the memory of Oliver's kisses still tingling on my lips, I allow myself to hope that maybe, just maybe, I've found someone I belong with too.

The secret of my donation to save Oliver's store, which had been burning inside me all evening, now feels like a warm glow in my chest. It's no longer just about saving a business. It's about preserving a piece of this community that I'm growing to love, about ensuring that the joy and warmth I've experienced tonight can continue for years to come.

As I drift off to sleep, my dreams are filled with twinkling lights, the sound of blades on ice, and the warmth of Oliver's smile.

And I can' t wait or tomorrow.

Twelve

REBECCA

The soft, ethereal glow of the Blessing Call Center beckons me as I step through its pearly gates. The familiar hum of angelic voices fills the air, a harmonious blend of requests and blessings that sends a tingle down my spine. It's been a while since I've been here, and I'd forgotten how... heavenly it feels.

I make my way past rows of gleaming white desks, each occupied by a Class B angel, their halo headest glowing softly as they coordinate blessings for their human charges. The gentle clatter of celestial keyboards and the whisper of wings create a soothing symphony of divine bureaucracy.

"Rebecca?" a familiar voice calls out. "Is that you?"

I turn to see Gladys, her gold curls bouncing as she waves me over. Her brown eyes sparkle with curiosity as I approach her desk.

"Hey, Gladys," I say, suddenly feeling a bit sheepish.

"I, uh, just wanted to stop by and say thanks. You know, for those boots you sent for Chloe."

Gladys's face lights up with a smile that could outshine the stars. "Oh, it was my pleasure. How did they work out?"

I can't help but grin as I think about Chloe traipsing around Benton Falls in those cozy, stylish boots. "They were perfect. You should've seen her face when she tried them on. I think it was the first time she actually enjoyed walking around town instead of complaining about her designer heels sinking into the snow."

Gladys laughs, the sound like tinkling bells. "I'm so glad to hear that. You know, it's rarely we get to see the direct impact of our blessings. It's nice to know they're making a difference."

I nod, a warm feeling spreading through my chest. It's moments like these that make me appreciate my role as a guardian angel in training, even if I sometimes miss my old life of luxury and achievement.

"So, how's the assignment going?" Gladys asks, leaning forward conspiratorially. "Word around the celestial water cooler is that you might be on track for your wings soon."

I feel a flutter of excitement at her words. "Really? I mean, I think it's going well. Chloe's definitely changed a lot since I started working with her. She's opening up, getting involved in the community. She even volunteered at a book fair."

Gladys's eyes widen. "Wow, that is progress. And

what about her relationship with that Oliver fellow? Any developments there?"

I'm about to answer when a gentle chime resonates through the call center. Gladys sighs, straightening up. "Duty calls. But hey, keep up the good work, Rebecca. I have a feeling we'll be seeing you with wings before you know it."

As I make my way out of the Blessing Call Center, I can't help but feel a surge of pride. Maybe Gladys is right. Maybe I am on track to earn my wings. The thought sends a thrill through me, making my steps lighter as I exit into the main celestial concourse.

The sight that greets me never fails to take my breath away, even after all this time. The vast expanse of heaven stretches out before me, a shimmering tapestry of stars and swirling galaxies. The air is filled with a soft, golden light that seems to emanate from everything and nothing all at once. In the distance, I can hear the faint strains of the angelic choir practicing their Christmas cantata.

I'm so lost in the beauty of it all that I almost bump into Henry, who seems to have appeared out of thin air.

"Whoa there, Rebecca," he says, his eyes twinkling with amusement. "Lost in thought, are we?"

I feel my cheeks flush. Even after all this time, Henry has a way of making me feel like a fledgling angel on my first day of training. "Sorry, Henry. I was just... taking it all in, I guess."

Henry nods, his silver hair catching the celestial light. "It is quite a sight, isn't it? No matter how long you've been here, it never loses its wonder." He pauses, studying me with those all-knowing eyes of his. "But I sense there's something else on your mind. Care to share?"

I hesitate for a moment, then decide to just go for it. "Well, I was just at the Blessing Call Center, thanking Gladys for those boots she sent to Chloe. And she mentioned... she said the angels are talking about me, maybe earning my wings soon. Is that true?"

Henry's expression softens, a gentle smile playing at his lips. "Well, you tell me, how do you think Chloe is doing?"

I feel a surge of excitement as I think about all the progress Chloe has made. "Oh, Henry, she's doing so well. You should see her. She's really embracing the spirit of Benton Falls. She volunteered at the Elementary School Book Fair, can you believe it? And she's been spending so much time with Oliver and the community. Those boots Gladys sent really did the trick—Chloe's been much more willing to explore the town now that her feet aren't freezing in those ridiculous designer heels."

Henry chuckles, the sound warm and rich. "That's wonderful to hear, Rebecca. And what about Oliver's store? I hear there have been some developments there."

I furrow my brow, confused. "Oliver's store? What do you mean?"

Henry's eyes twinkle mischievously. "Oh, you haven't heard? It seems Chloe made quite a generous gesture. She anonymously donated a substantial sum to save the department store."

My jaw drops. "She what? But... but how? When? I knew nothing about this."

Henry laughs, patting my shoulder. "Sometimes, Rebecca, our charges surprise us. They make choices we didn't expect, grow in ways we couldn't have imagined. That's the beauty of free will—and the challenge of being a guardian angel."

I'm reeling from this revelation. Chloe, my stubborn, money-obsessed Chloe, made an anonymous donation? To save Oliver's store? It seems impossible, and yet... a warm feeling spreads through my chest. Pride, I realize. I'm proud of her.

"That's... that's amazing," I say, still trying to wrap my head around it. "I can't believe she did that. Henry, does this mean... am I done? Have I completed my assignment?"

The hope in my voice is embarrassingly obvious, but I can't help it. The thought of finally earning my wings, of proving myself as a veritable guardian angel, is almost overwhelming.

But Henry's expression turns serious, and I feel my heart sink. "Rebecca," he says gently, "you've done excellent work with Chloe. She's grown tremendously, and you should be very proud of that. But..."

"But?" I prompt, trying to keep the disappointment out of my voice.

Henry sighs, his eyes full of compassion. "But there's still work to be done. Chloe's journey isn't over yet, and neither is yours."

I feel like I've been doused with cold water. "What? But Henry, she's changed so much. She's volunteering, she's connecting with people, she made that donation... what more is there?"

Henry places a hand on my shoulder, his touch warm and comforting. "Rebecca, being a guardian angel isn't just about changing someone's actions. It's about transforming their heart. Chloe has made great strides, but there are still wounds that need healing, truths she needs to face."

I slump, feeling deflated. "So... what do I do now?"

Henry's smile is gentle but firm. "You keep going. You stay by her side. And most importantly, you trust the process. Remember, Rebecca, this journey isn't just about Chloe. It's about you, too. There are still lessons for you to learn, growth for you to experience."

I nod, trying to push down my disappointment. "I understand. Thank you, Henry."

As Henry turns to leave, a thought strikes me. "Wait. Henry, what exactly do I need to do? What work is left?"

But Henry just smiles enigmatically. "That, my dear Rebecca, is something you'll have to figure out for yourself. Trust your instincts. And remember, sometimes the greatest miracles happen when we least expect them."

With that, he vanishes in a soft shimmer of light, leaving me standing alone in the celestial concourse, my mind whirling with questions.

I make my way to the edge of the heavenly realm, where the boundary between Earth and Heaven is thinnest. As I prepare to teleport back to Benton Falls, I can't shake the feeling that something big is coming—

Something that will test both Chloe and me in ways we can't imagine.

Thirteen

CHLOE

Snowflakes dust the air as Oliver and I make our way into the Benton Falls High School auditorium. The familiar mixture of excitement and nerves that always precede a theatrical performance buzzes around us, amplified by the cheerful chatter of parents, students, and community members finding their seats.

"I can't believe you talked me into this," I mutter to Oliver, adjusting the soft wool scarf around my neck. It's one I picked up at the Christmas market, much to my surprise. A month ago, I wouldn't have been caught dead in anything not bearing a designer label.

Oliver grins, his hazel eyes twinkling with amusement. "Come on, Chloe. 'It's a Wonderful Life' is a classic. Plus, these kids have worked really hard on the play. It'll be fun, I promise."

I roll my eyes, but there's no real annoyance behind it. The truth is, I'm actually looking forward to this. The realization startles me a little. When did I start enjoying small-town activities like high school plays? Probably has something to do with all the concerts I've been to.

We find our seats near the front, the plush velvet chairs adorned with festive red and green cushions. As we settle in, I can't help but notice how perfectly Oliver fits into this scene. He greets everyone around us by name, asking after family members and complimenting holiday outfits. The easy way he connects with people still amazes me.

The lights dim, and a hush falls over the audience. The curtain rises to reveal a meticulously crafted set of Bedford Falls. I have to admit, I'm impressed. The quaint Main Street scene, complete with gently falling snow and softly glowing streetlights, captures the nostalgic charm of the beloved classic perfectly.

As the play unfolds, I find myself drawn into the story of George Bailey. The student playing him throws himself into the role with admirable enthusiasm, capturing George's frustrations and dreams with surprising depth for a high schooler.

When George contemplates ending his life on the bridge, I feel a lump form in my throat. The despair in his voice, the feeling of being trapped and worthless... it hits closer to home than I'd like to admit. I think back to my life just a few weeks ago, how empty and meaningless it felt despite all my success.

Oliver must sense my discomfort because he reaches over and takes my hand, giving it a gentle squeeze. The warmth of his touch anchors me, reminding me I'm not alone anymore.

As Clarence the angel shows George the impact he's had on the lives of others, I feel something shift inside me. Every small act of kindness, every moment of connection that George thought insignificant, had rippled out to change the entire town. It's a powerful message, one that resonates deeply with the changes I've been experiencing in Benton Falls.

By the time the entire town rallies to help George in his moment of need, tears are streaming down my face. I'm not alone; I can hear sniffles and see people dabbing at their eyes all around me. The student actors pour their hearts into the ending scene, their voices rising in a heartfelt rendition of "Auld Lang Syne" that fills the auditorium with a palpable sense of joy and community.

As the curtain falls and the audience erupts into thunderous applause, I turn to Oliver, suddenly self-conscious about my tear-stained cheeks. But the look in his eyes stops any attempt at composure. He's looking at me with such tenderness, such understanding, that it takes my breath away.

"You okay?" he asks softly, his thumb gently wiping away a stray tear.

I nod, not trusting my voice just yet. Oliver seems to understand, wrapping an arm around my shoulders as we stand to join the standing ovation.

After the play, we linger in the lobby, sipping hot chocolate from paper cups as we wait for the crowd to thin out. The air is filled with excited chatter as people discuss their favorite parts of the performance.

"So," Oliver says, a hint of teasing in his voice, "still think I was crazy for dragging you to a high school play?"

I laugh, the sound lighter and more carefree than I can ever remember it being. "Okay, okay, you were right. It was... it was really beautiful, actually. Those kids did an amazing job."

Oliver's smile softens. "They really did. You know, watching it tonight... it reminded me of why I love this town so much. Everyone coming together, supporting each other. It's special, you know?"

I nod, understanding dawning. "It's like Bedford Falls. Everyone knows everyone, cares about everyone. It's... it's wonderful." The word feels strange on my tongue, but right somehow.

We step outside into the chilly night air. The surrounding neighborhood is lit up with twinkling Christmas lights, casting a warm glow over the freshly fallen snow. It looks like something out of a postcard, almost too perfect to be real.

"Want to take a walk?" Oliver asks, offering me his arm.

I loop my arm through his without hesitation. "I'd love to."

As we stroll through the quiet streets, our breath visible in the cold air, I open up to Oliver in a way I never have before.

"You know," I say softly, "when George was on that bridge, feeling like his life had no meaning... I understood that. A few weeks ago, before I came here, that's how I felt all the time, even though I never recognized it."

Oliver stops walking, turning to face me. His expression is a mixture of concern and compassion that makes my heart ache. "Chloe..."

I shake my head, needing to get this out. "I had everything I thought I wanted. Success, money, power. But it was all... empty. I felt so alone, so disconnected from everything and everyone. Coming here, meeting you, being part of this community... it's shown me what really matters."

Oliver pulls me into a hug, and I melt into his embrace. The solid warmth of him, the scent of pine and something uniquely Oliver, wraps around me like a cocoon of safety and acceptance.

"I'm so glad you're here," he murmurs into my hair. "You've brought so much to this town, Chloe. To me."

We stand there for a long moment, just holding each other under the gently falling snow. When we finally pull apart, Oliver's eyes are shining with an emotion I'm not quite ready to name.

"Come on," he says, taking my hand. "There's something I want to show you."

He leads me to his store, unlocking the door and guiding me inside. The familiar scent of leather and wood polish greets us, along with the lingering aroma of the cinnamon pinecones that decorate the counter.

Oliver flips on the lights, revealing the store decked out in full Christmas splendor. Garlands drape from the rafters, twinkling lights wind around display cases, and a majestic Christmas tree stands proudly in the corner.

"It's beautiful," I breathe, taking it all in.

Oliver's smile is a mixture of pride and something softer, more vulnerable. "Chloe, I have some news. Something amazing has happened."

I feel my heart rate pick up. Does he know about my donation?

"Someone made an anonymous donation to the store," Oliver says, his voice filled with wonder. "A really substantial one. With this money, and some ideas you've given me about modernizing our operations... I think we can keep the store going. Not just surviving, but thriving."

The joy in his voice, the hope shining in his eyes, makes my own eyes fill with tears again. I did this. I helped make this happen.

"Oliver, that's wonderful," I say, my voice thick with emotion.

He nods, running a hand through his hair in that endearing way he does when he's excited. "It is. And you know what? It's made me realize something. This store, this town... it's not just about preserving the past. It's about building a future. A future where tradition and innovation can coexist, where we can honor our history while still moving forward."

I listen, captivated, as Oliver outlines his vision for the store. He talks about introducing an online component to reach a wider customer base, about partnering with local artisans to showcase their work, about hosting community events to bring people together.

"And Chloe," he says, taking both my hands in his, "I want you to be part of it. Your business acumen, your fresh perspective... it's exactly what this place needs. What I need."

I'm speechless for a moment, overwhelmed by the trust and faith he's placing in me. "Oliver, I... I don't know what to say."

He smiles, that warm, genuine smile that never fails to make my heart skip a beat. "Say you'll stay. Say you'll help me make this vision a reality."

The old Chloe, the one who arrived in Benton Falls just a few weeks ago, would have balked at the idea. She would have seen it as a step backward, a waste of her talents and ambition.

But this Chloe pauses... she sees it differently.

I see the possibility of a future here in Benton Falls. A future filled with purpose and love, with the satisfaction of building something meaningful. A future with Oliver.

The realization doesn't completely freak me out like I thought it would. Instead, it fills me with a sense of peace, of rightness.

"It's something to consider," I say with a smile. "Can you give me a little time to think everything through?"

The grin that breaks across Oliver's face is like the sun coming out from behind the clouds. "Of course." He pulls me close, and when our lips meet, it feels like coming home.

As we stand there in the glow of the Christmas lights, surrounded by the history and promise of Hanks' Department Store, I feel a profound sense of gratitude wash over me. Gratitude for this town that's welcomed me, for the experiences that have opened my heart, and for Oliver, who's shown me what it means to truly live and love.

I think back to George Bailey's revelation at the end of the play. Like him, I've been given a wonderful gift—the chance to see my life, and myself, in a new light. The chance to make a difference, to be part of something bigger than myself.

As Oliver and I leave the store hand in hand, stepping out into the snowy night, I'm filled with a sense of excitement for the future.

The next morning, I wake to the sound of carolers outside my window. For a moment, I'm disoriented, the events of last night feeling almost like a dream. But as I sit up, my eyes falling on the framed photo of Oliver and me from the ice skating rink, a warm smile spreads across my face. It wasn't a dream. This is my life now, and could always be, if I agree to stay in Benton Falls—all I have to do is decide.

But not today.

I throw on a cozy sweater and make my way downstairs, when the doorbell rings. I make my way to the door and open it. To my surprise, I find Rebecca there, humming softly as she arranges a plate of Christmas cookies.

"Rebecca?" I say, still not quite used to having an unintentional bestie. "What are you doing here?"

She tilts her head, her golden hair catching the

morning light. "Oh, good morning, Chloe. I hope you don't mind. I thought you might like some company this morning. And some of Maggie's famous gingerbread cookies."

I shake my head, oddly touched by the gesture. "No, I don't mind at all. Thank you."

Rebecca steps inside, and I lead her into the kitchen. Minutes later, the coffee is ready. As we sit at the kitchen table, sipping coffee and nibbling on cookies that taste like Christmas itself, I open up to Rebecca about last night. About the play, about Oliver's plans for the store, about my decision to stay in Benton Falls.

Rebecca listens attentively, her eyes sparkling with what looks suspiciously like pride. "Chloe, that's wonderful. I'm so happy for you. You know, when you first came to town, I never would have guessed things would turn out like this."

I laugh, the sound full and rich. "Believe me, neither did I. But now... I can't imagine it any other way."

As we continue to chat, the warmth of friendship and the joy of the season filling the kitchen, I'm struck by how much my life has changed in such a short time. Maybe it's not about the pursuit of money...

Later that day, as I help Oliver hang a "Happy Holidays" banner across the front of his store, I catch sight of my reflection in the window. The woman looking back at me is almost unrecognizable from the cold, ambitious CEO who arrived in Benton Falls just weeks ago.

This Chloe has rosy cheeks from the cold and exertion, her hair slightly mussed from the wind. But more than that, her eyes are bright with happiness, her smile genuine and warm. This Chloe looks alive in a way I haven't felt in years.

"Penny for your thoughts?" Oliver asks, coming up behind me and wrapping his arms around my waist.

I lean back into him, savoring the solid warmth of his presence. "Just thinking about how different everything is. How different I am."

"Oh?" Oliver presses a soft kiss to my temple. "Different in a good way, I hope?"

I turn in his arms, meeting his gaze. "The best way. Oliver, I... I'm happier than I've ever been. And it's because of you, because of this town. You've shown me what really matters in life."

The light shining in Oliver's eyes takes my breath away. He cares about me. "You've changed me too, Chloe. You've brought a fresh energy to this place, pushed me to think bigger. We make a good team, you and I."

The sound of children's laughter draws our attention. A group of kids is having a snowball fight in the town square, their shrieks of delight filling the air. Without thinking, I scoop up a handful of snow and lob it playfully at Oliver.

His look of shock quickly gives way to a mischievous grin. "Oh, it's on, Anderson."

What follows is the most fun I've had in years. We chase each other around the square, lobbing snowballs and laughing like children. I'm breathless and soaked, my carefully styled hair a mess, but I've never felt more alive.

Oliver pulls me close, his breath warm against my cold cheek. "You know," he says softly, "I think this is going to be the best Christmas Benton Falls has ever seen."

As I look out at the town, at the twinkling lights and the smiling faces of people going about their day, at the sense of community and warmth that permeates every corner, I can't help but agree.

"You're right," I say, snuggling closer to him. "It really is a wonderful life."

And as we sit there, watching the snow fall and planning our future together, I silently thank whatever twist of fate brought me to this magical little town. Because here, in Benton Falls, I've found more than just a place to belong. I've found myself.

Fourteen

CHLOE

The soft glow of candlelight dances across the polished wood pews as Oliver and I make our way into the church. The scent of pine and citrus envelops us, mingling with the familiar musty sweetness of well-worn hymnals and decades of faithful worship. It's a comforting smell, one that reminds me of childhood Christmases spent here with my grandmother.

"It's beautiful," I whisper to Oliver, my eyes drawn to the magnificent Christmas tree near the altar. Its twinkling lights reflect in the stained-glass windows, creating a kaleidoscope of colors that seems almost magical.

Oliver squeezes my hand, his smile warm in the flickering light. "Wait till you see the pageant. The kids have been practicing for weeks."

We find seats near the front, settling in among the other townspeople. The excited chatter of children and the soft murmur of adult conversations fill the air, creating a festive atmosphere that wraps around me like a cozy blanket.

As we wait for the pageant to begin, I find myself marveling at how comfortable I feel here. Just a few weeks ago, the thought of attending a small-town church pageant would have filled me with dread. Now, sitting here with Oliver, surrounded by people who have welcomed me so warmly into their community, I can't imagine being anywhere else.

The soft strains of "O Come, All Ye Faithful" signal the start of the pageant. The congregation falls silent as the first notes of the organ fill the church. Down the aisle comes a procession of children dressed as angels, shepherds, and wise men. Their faces are a mix of solemn concentration and barely contained excitement.

I feel Oliver's arm slip around my shoulders, and I lean into him, savoring the warmth of his presence. As we watch the timeless story of Christ's birth unfold before us, I'm struck by the simplicity and power of the message. A child, born in the humblest of circumstances, bringing hope and love to the world.

The little girl playing Mary cradles the baby Jesus with such tenderness that I feel a lump form in my throat. It's a stark reminder of the purity of a child's love, untainted by the complexities and fears that we adults so often let cloud our hearts.

As the pageant progresses, I find myself drawn more and more into the spirit of the season. The children's earnest performances, the familiar carols sung with heartfelt enthusiasm by the congregation, the sense of community and shared joy that permeates the air – it all combines to create a feeling of belonging that I've never experienced before.

When the final notes of "Silent Night" fade away, I realize there are tears in my eyes. Oliver notices, gently wiping away a stray tear with his thumb.

"You okay?" he whispers, concern evident in his voice.

I nod, offering him a watery smile. "More than okay. It's just... I've never felt anything like this before. It's beautiful."

Oliver's answering smile is radiant. "That's the magic of Christmas in Benton Falls. It has a way of touching your heart when you least expect it."

As we file out of the church after the pageant, the cold night air nips at our cheeks, a stark contrast to the warmth inside. But the chill does nothing to dampen the glow of joy I feel inside.

Oliver and I linger on the church steps, watching as families and friends exchange hugs and holiday wishes. The sound of laughter and cheerful conversation fills the air, punctuated by the distant chiming of bells from the town square.

"So," Oliver says, a hint of teasing in his voice, "what did you think of the pageant?"

I pretend to consider for a moment. "Well, I have to say, it was much better than any Broadway show I've seen lately."

Oliver laughs, the sound rich and warm. "High praise indeed from a big city girl."

As we walk back towards the town square, our hands intertwined, I open up to Oliver about the thoughts swirling in my mind.

"You know," I begin, "being here, seeing how this community comes together... it's made me think about the future. About how I might contribute more." I glance up at him. "To Benton Falls."

Oliver's eyes light up with interest. "Oh? What ideas do you have?"

I feel a flutter of excitement as I share the plans that have been forming in my mind. "Well, I've been thinking about ways to invest in the town to help revive some of the local businesses. Maybe set up a fund for small business loans, or create a mentorship program for young entrepreneurs."

As I talk, I can feel my old business acumen kicking in, but it's different now. Instead of focusing solely on profit margins and market shares, I'm thinking about community impact and sustainable growth.

"And of course," I continue, caught up in my enthusiasm, "I'd want to do more for specific businesses too. Like what I did for your store—"

I freeze, realizing what I've just said. Oliver's brow furrows in confusion.

"What you did for my store?" he asks slowly. "What do you mean, Chloe?"

My heart races as I scramble to backtrack. "I just meant... you know, helping with the toy drive and all that..."

But Oliver's not buying it. His eyes narrow, and I can see the moment realization dawns on him.

"Chloe," he says, his voice unnervingly calm, "are you saying you're the one who made that anonymous donation to the store?"

I swallow hard, knowing there's no way out of this now. "I... yes. Yes, I am."

For a moment, Oliver just stares at me, his expression unreadable. Then, to my horror, I see a flash of anger in his eyes.

"You what?" he says, his voice low and tight. He steps back, breaking our embrace, and I feel a chill that has nothing to do with the winter air.

"I thought... I wanted to help," I stammer, suddenly uncertain. This isn't the reaction I expected at all.

Oliver runs a hand through his hair, a gesture I recognize as a sign of frustration. "Help? Chloe, I don't need your charity. I don't need your pity."

"It's not pity." I protest, feeling a knot of anxiety form in my stomach. "I care about you, about the store. I just wanted to contribute."

"By going behind my back?" Oliver's voice is rising now, drawing curious glances from passersby. "By not being honest with me? Do you have any idea how that makes me feel?"

I reach out to him, but he steps back again. "Oliver, please, I didn't mean to upset you. I thought you'd be happy."

He shakes his head, his expression a mixture of hurt and disappointment that cuts me to the core. "Happy?

To find out that the woman I'm falling in love with has been lying to me? To realize that she thinks I can't handle my business without her swooping in to save the day?"

His words hit me like a physical blow. Falling in love? But before I can process that, he's turning away.

"I need some time to think," he says, his voice cold in a way I've never heard before. "Goodnight, Chloe."

And then he's gone, striding away across the square, leaving me standing alone in the snow, the weight of my well-intentioned secret crushing down on me.

For a long moment, I just stand there, too shocked to move. The cheerful Christmas lights and the distant sound of carols now seem to mock me, a stark contrast to the ache in my chest.

As the reality of what just happened sinks in, I feel a familiar anger rising within me. How dare he? How dare he make me feel this way when all I was trying to do was help?

I turn on my heel, marching back towards my grandmother's house with quick, angry steps. The snow crunches beneath my feet, each step punctuated by a swirl of emotions—hurt, betrayal, indignation.

By the time I reach the house, I'm fuming. I slam the door behind me; the sound echoing through the quiet rooms. Throwing my coat onto a chair, I storm into the living room, pacing back and forth in front of the fireplace.

"Stupid, naïve Chloe," I mutter to myself, angry tears pricking at my eyes. "Thinking you could play small-town hero. Thinking you could actually belong here."

The cynical voice in my head, the one I thought I'd silenced, comes roaring back to life. See? This happens when you let people in. When you make yourself vulnerable. You get hurt. You get left behind.

I sink onto the couch, burying my face in my hands. The memory of Oliver's hurt and angry expression plays on repeat in my mind, each replay like a knife twisting in my gut.

But as the initial shock wears off, my sadness gives way to a burning anger. Who does Oliver think he is? I was only trying to help, to secure the future of his precious store. And this is how he repays me? With accusations and cold shoulders?

I stand up abruptly, my fists clenched at my sides. "Fine," I say out loud to the empty room. "If that's how he wants it, that's how it'll be."

I stride over to the window, looking out at the snow-covered street. The twinkling Christmas lights that had seemed so magical just hours ago now look gaudy and artificial.

This is exactly why I don't let people in, why I've always kept my emotions in check. Because in the end, everyone leaves. Everyone disappoints you.

Well, not this time. This time, I won't be the one left behind. I won't be the one nursing a broken heart while Oliver plays the wronged party.

No, I decide, my jaw set in determination. I'm done. Done with Oliver, done with this town, done with this whole ridiculous Christmas fantasy.

I don't need the approval of some small-town shop-

141

keeper or the acceptance of a community that clearly doesn't understand me.

As I turn away from the window, my eyes fall on the gifts piled under the Christmas tree—presents for Oliver, for Rebecca, for the various townspeople I've grown close to. With a surge of bitter satisfaction, I gather them up.

I'll return them all tomorrow. Or better yet, I'll donate them to charity. Let someone else benefit from my misguided attempt at playing Santa Claus.

As I stack the gifts in a corner, a small part of me whispers that I'm overreacting, that I should calm down and try to see things from Oliver's perspective. But I squash that voice ruthlessly. I've spent too much of my life trying to understand others, trying to make myself small and acceptable. Not anymore.

I march up to my room, pulling out my suitcase from the closet. I'll leave first thing in the morning, I decide. Back to the city, back to my real life. Back to a world where I'm in control, where I don't have to worry about messy emotions or small-town drama.

As I pack, I feel a grim satisfaction. This is what I get for letting my guard down, for thinking I could change. Well, lesson learned.

Benton Falls can keep its Christmas cheer and its quaint traditions. Oliver can keep his store and his pride. I don't need any of it.

I pause in my packing, catching sight of my reflection in the mirror. My cheeks are flushed with anger, my eyes bright with unshed tears. But beneath that, I see something else—the strong, independent woman I've always been. The woman who doesn't need anyone's approval or love to succeed.

"Merry Christmas to me," I mutter sarcastically, turning away from the mirror.

As I climb into bed, my mind is made up. Tomorrow, I'll leave Benton Falls behind. I'll go back to my life in the city, back to the world I understand. A world where success is measured in dollars and cents, not in small-town goodwill.

And if there's an ache in my chest, a sense of loss that threatens to overwhelm me? Well, I'll just have to ignore it. Because Chloe Anderson doesn't get her heart broken. Not by anyone, and certainly not by Oliver Hanks.

With that thought, I turn off the light, letting the darkness envelop me. Tomorrow is another day. A day to reclaim my old life, my old self. A day to leave behind this Christmas fantasy once and for all.

As I drift off to sleep, I try to ignore the faint sound of carolers in the distance, their cheerful voices a stark counterpoint to the anger and hurt swirling inside me. Instead, I focus on the future—a future without Benton Falls, without Oliver, without the vulnerability that comes with letting people in.

It's better this way, I tell myself firmly. Safer. And if a small part of me mourns the loss of the warmth and belonging I've found here? Well, that's just a price I'll have to pay for protecting myself.

After all, isn't that what I've always done best? Protect myself, no matter the cost.

Fifteen

REBECCA

I'm standing on Chloe's front porch, my golden hair catching the early morning sunlight. I can't help but grin, thinking about the romantic evening Chloe and Oliver must have shared at the church pageant last night. My wings are practically quivering with anticipation—not that I have actual wings yet, but a girl can dream, right?

I take a deep breath, inhaling the scent of evergreen and spice, which seems to permeate everything in Benton Falls during the holiday season. The porch is dusted with a light layer of snow, and icicles glisten from the eaves, creating a picturesque winter wonderland.

Straightening my fuzzy white sweater—because even angels need to look cute while blending in—I reach out to knock on the deep green front door. The wreath, adorned with red berries and an enormous bow, sways gently with the motion.

"Chloe?" I call out cheerfully. "It's Rebecca."

I hear shuffling inside, and then the door swings open. My cheerful smile freezes on my face as I take in the sight before me.

Chloe looks... well, let's just say she doesn't look like a woman who spent a romantic evening at a church pageant. Her usually impeccable hair is a mess, her eyes are red-rimmed, and she's wearing what appears to be an oversized sweatshirt with "I'd Rather Be Working" emblazoned across the front. It's about as far from her usual polished appearance as you can get.

"Rebecca," she says, her voice flat. "What are you doing here?"

I blink, thrown off balance. This isn't the Chloe I've come to know over the past few weeks. This Chloe reminds me of the cold, independent woman who first arrived in Benton Falls. It's like watching all my hard work unravel before my eyes.

"I... uh...?" I stammer, "I mean, I thought I'd stop by and see how your evening went. The pageant was beautiful, wasn't it?"

Chloe's eyes narrow, and I feel a chill that has nothing to do with the winter air. "The pageant," she says flatly. "Right. Why don't you come in, Rebecca? I think we need to talk."

As I step inside, the warmth of the house wraps around me, but it does little to dispel the sense of unease growing in the pit of my stomach. The living room, which had seemed so cozy and festive just yesterday, now feels oppressive. The twinkling lights of the Christmas tree seem to mock me, reminding me of how quickly things can change.

Chloe leads me to the kitchen, where the scent of coffee hangs heavy in the air. She pours herself a cup, not offering me one. Not that I need caffeine, being an angel and all, but still. Rude.

"So," she says, leaning against the counter and fixing me with a steely gaze. "You want to know how my evening went?"

I nod, not trusting myself to speak. My empathic abilities are going haywire, picking up waves of anger, hurt, and... is that fear? Oh boy, what happened last night?

Chloe takes a deep breath, then launches into her story. She tells me about the pageant, about her conversation with Oliver afterward, about her accidental revelation of the anonymous donation. With each word, I feel my hopes for a quick and easy wing-earning sinking lower and lower.

"And then," Chloe says, her voice bitter, "he just left. Walked away like I'd committed some terrible crime. All because I tried to help."

I stand there, stunned. This is not how it was supposed to go. They were supposed to fall in love, realize the true meaning of Christmas, and live happily ever after. That's how these things work, right?

"Chloe," I say carefully, "I'm sure Oliver was just surprised. If you talk to him—"

"Talk to him?" Chloe interrupts, her eyes flashing.

"Why should I? He made his feelings pretty clear. And you know what? He's right. I was a fool."

"A fool?" I echo, a sinking feeling in my stomach.

Chloe nods, her jaw set in a determined line. "A fool to think I could fit in here. A fool to get caught up in all this... this Christmas nonsense. A fool to think I should care about others more than myself."

Each word feels like a physical blow. I watch as Chloe paces the kitchen, dismantling weeks of progress in a matter of minutes. The warm, caring woman I knew is disappearing before my eyes, replaced by the cold, hard businesswoman who first arrived in Benton Falls.

"I'm leaving," Chloe announces, turning to face me. "I'm going back to the city, back to my real life. This whole Benton Falls adventure was a mistake."

For a moment, I'm too shocked to speak. Then, to my surprise, I feel a surge of anger. All my hard work, all the progress Chloe has made, and she's just going to throw it away? Oh heck no.

"Now wait just a minute," I say, my voice sharper than I intend. "You can't just leave. What about Oliver? What about the town? What about all the good you've done here?"

Chloe's laugh is harsh and bitter. "Good? What good? I tried to help, and look where it got me. No, Rebecca. I'm done playing small-town angel. I'm going back to where I belong."

As I watch Chloe turn away, reaching for her phone to presumably book a flight, I feel a moment of panic. This can't be happening. I can't fail. I can't lose my chance at wings. I can't let Chloe throw away her chance at happiness.

And then, like a bolt of divine inspiration, it hits me. This. This is what Henry was talking about. The work that still needed to be done. It wasn't about getting Chloe and Oliver together or making Chloe love Christmas. It was about this moment, this test of faith and love.

I take a deep breath, forcing myself to really look at Chloe. Not with my eyes, but with my heart. And what I see nearly takes my breath away.

Beneath the anger, beneath the cold exterior, I see a desperate, frightened woman. A woman who's been hurt so many times that she's terrified of letting anyone in. A woman who's so afraid of losing control that she'd rather push everyone away than risk being vulnerable.

In that moment, I feel a wave of empathy so strong it almost brings me to my tears. Because I recognize that woman. She's me. Or at least, she's who I used to be.

"Chloe," I say softly, all my anger draining away. "I know you're hurt. I know you're scared. But running away isn't the answer."

Chloe's head snaps up, her eyes meeting mine. For a moment, I see a flicker of something—hope? fear?—before her walls slam back into place.

"You know nothing about me," she says, but her voice lacks conviction.

I take a step closer, wishing I could wrap my wings around her. Oh right, no wings yet. Maybe a hug will do?

"I know more than you think," I say gently. "I know what it's like to be afraid of letting people in. To think that success and money are the only things that matter. But Chloe, there's so much more to life than that. And you've seen it here in Benton Falls."

Chloe's lower lip trembles, and I can see her resolve wavering. "It doesn't matter," she whispers. "I've ruined everything. Oliver hates me."

I shake my head, reaching out to take her hand. To my surprise, she doesn't pull away. "You haven't ruined anything. I'm not sure why Oliver is so upset, but giving a gift out of love and generosity isn't something to be ashamed of."

As I speak, I can feel something shifting in the air around us. It's like the entire universe is holding its breath, waiting to see what Chloe will do next.

"I don't know how to fix this," Chloe admits, and the vulnerability in her voice makes my heart ache.

"You don't have to do it alone," I tell her, squeezing her hand. "That's what friends are for. That's what community is for. And whether or not you believe it, you have both things here in Benton Falls."

For a long moment, Chloe is silent. I can practically see the gears turning in her head, weighing her options, battling her fears. Then, slowly, she shakes her head. "No. I'm leaving." She sighs. "It's better this way."

"But Chloe—" I interject.

"No," she shakes her head again. "It's better if I go back to Boston." Chloe's eyes are brimming with emotion and I don't know what to do, but she solves that issue for me with her next command. "It's time for you to go. I've still got some packing to do."

And just like that. I'm dismissed and destined to be a useless heavenly weather forecaster forever.

As Chloe shuts the door, I stand on the porch, my mind racing. This is a total disaster. Chloe's not willing to try, and Oliver's still hurt and angry. How am I supposed to fix this?

I close my eyes, reaching out with my angelic senses. I can feel the swirl of emotions in the town – the excitement of children looking forward to Christmas, the stress of adults trying to get everything done, the warmth of love and friendship that seems to permeate every corner of Benton Falls. And underneath it all, I sense two distinct threads of pain and longing—Chloe and Oliver, both hurting, both wanting to reach out but held back by fear and pride.

"Oh, for heaven's sake," I mutter to myself. "Why do humans have to be so complicated?"

As if in answer to my question, I feel a familiar presence in the vicinity. I open my eyes to see Henry sitting on the porch bench, his silver hair slightly mussed and his blue eyes twinkling with amusement.

"Having some trouble, Rebecca?" he asks, his voice gentle.

I sigh, slumping back against the couch. "Henry, this is a disaster. Chloe and Oliver had a fight, Chloe's leaving town, and now I have no idea how to fix things. I thought I was doing so well, and now... now I feel like I'm right back where I started."

Henry nods sagely, stroking his beard. "Ah, but are you really? Think about it, Rebecca. How would you have reacted to this situation when you first started your assignment?"

I pause, considering. "I... I probably would have been angry. Frustrated that Chloe was messing up my chances of earning my wings. I might have even given up."

"And now?" Henry prompts.

"Now," I say slowly, realization dawning, "now I just want to help. I want Chloe to be happy, to find love, to understand the true meaning of Christmas. I don't care about my wings—well, okay, I care a little—but it's not the most important thing anymore."

Henry's smile is warm and proud. "Exactly. You've grown, Rebecca. You've learned to put others before yourself, to see beyond the surface to the heart of what really matters. That's what being a guardian angel is all about."

I feel a warmth spreading through me at his words. He's right. I have changed. The Rebecca who first arrived in Benton Falls wouldn't recognize the angel I've become.

"So what do I do now?" I ask, feeling a renewed sense of determination.

Henry's eyes twinkle mischievously. "Well, you could always call in a favor from our friends in the Cupid department."

I stare at him, my jaw dropping. "Wait, that's a real thing? We can do that?"

Henry chuckles. "Of course it's real. Where do you think all those romantic holiday movies get their inspiration from? But I don't think you need reinforcements just yet. And you've still got your Miracle Card, right?"

I nod, my mind already racing with possibilities. Which miracle do I ask for? "Chloe and Oliver love each other. They're just... stuck. Afraid. Just need a little push."

"Perhaps," Henry says, standing up. "But remember, the choice is ultimately theirs. We can guide, we can inspire, but we can't force. That's the beauty and the challenge of free will."

Ugh. "Free will," I mutter. "It's great until it applies to my assignment."

Henry chuckles. "You're not the first angel in training with those sentiments." He waves and then disappears, leaving me alone with a seemingly impossible challenge. But I smile. After all, I've got a Miracle Card in my back pocket.

Sixteen

CHLOE

The gentle hum of my laptop fills the quiet living room as I finish booking my flight back to Boston. The cursor hovers over the 'Confirm' button, and I feel a twinge of... something. Regret? Relief? I'm not sure anymore. With a decisive click, it's done. In just a few hours, I'll be leaving Benton Falls behind.

I close my laptop and look around the room. The cheerful Christmas decorations that had seemed so magical just days ago now feel like they're mocking me. The twinkling lights of the tree reflect in the window, blurring with the falling snow outside. It's beautiful, I have to admit, but it no longer fills me with the warmth it once did.

A knock at the door startles me from my thoughts. I consider ignoring it, but the knocking persists, growing more insistent. With a sigh, I heave myself off the couch and make my way to the door.

"Rebecca," I say flatly as I open it, not at all surprised

to see my overly cheerful neighbor standing there, a bright smile on her face despite the cold. Apparently, she doesn't know how to use a cell phone.

"Chloe." she exclaims, her breath visible in the frosty air. "I'm so glad I caught you. I need a huge favor."

I raise an eyebrow, already feeling myself being pulled into whatever scheme Rebecca has cooked up. "Rebecca, I'm leaving in a few hours. My flight—"

"I know, I know," she interrupts, her eyes pleading. "But this won't take long, I promise. We need help with the Last Day of School Christmas party at the elementary school. Mrs. Carson came down with the flu, and we're short-handed. Please, Chloe? The kids will be so disappointed if we have to cancel."

I open my mouth to refuse, but something in Rebecca's expression stops me. Maybe it's the sincerity in her eyes, or maybe it's just that I'm tired of feeling angry and bitter. Whatever it is, I find myself nodding.

"Fine," I say with a sigh. "But just for an hour or two. I can't miss my flight."

Rebecca's face lights up like the Christmas tree behind me. "Thank you, Chloe. You're a lifesaver. I promise you won't regret this."

As I grab my coat and follow Rebecca out into the snow-covered street, I can't help but think that I'm probably going to regret this very much.

The elementary school is a whirlwind of activity when we arrive. The hallways are decked with paper chains and children's artwork, the scent of sugar cookies and pine needles filling the air. It's chaos, but there's a joyful energy to it that even I can't deny.

"Okay," Rebecca says, steering me towards a classroom. "You'll be helping in Ms. Carson's second-grade class. Just keep the kids entertained, help with the gift exchange, that sort of thing. You'll do great."

Before I can protest, she's gone, leaving me standing in front of a door decorated with construction paper reindeer and snowflakes. Taking a deep breath, I push it open.

Twenty pairs of eyes turn to look at me as I enter. The classroom is a riot of red and green, with twinkling lights strung across the ceiling and a small Christmas tree in the corner. The kids are seated at their desks, which are covered in glitter and half-finished crafts.

"Um, hello," I say, feeling wildly out of my depth. "I'm Ms. Anderson. I'll be helping with your party today."

There's a moment of silence, and then a little girl in the front row pipes up. "Are you a Christmas angel?"

I blink, taken aback. "What? No, I'm just... I'm a friend of Ms. Carson's." The lie feels strange on my tongue, but I figure it's easier than explaining the truth.

"Oh," the girl says, looking a bit disappointed. "Well, can you do magic?"

A chuckle escapes me before I can stop it. "Sorry, no magic. But I hear we have some fun activities planned. Shall we get started?"

The next hour passes in a blur of activity. We play "Pin the Nose on Rudolph," decorate cookies, and sing carols. I'm surprised to find that I remember most of the words, memories of childhood Christmases with my grandmother surfacing unbidden.

As we're cleaning up from the cookie decorating, a small hand tugs on my sleeve. I look down to see the same little girl from earlier, her big brown eyes serious.

"Ms. Anderson," she says solemnly, "I made this for you." She holds out a slightly misshapen cookie, covered in a mountain of sprinkles and icing.

For a moment, I'm speechless. "For me?" I finally manage. "But... why?"

She shrugs, a gap-toothed smile spreading across her face. "Because you looked sad when you came in. Mommy says cookies make everything better."

I take the cookie carefully, something warm and unfamiliar blooming in my chest. "Thank you," I say softly. "That's very kind of you."

The little girl beams at me before skipping off to join her friends. I stand there, holding the cookie, feeling like something fundamental has shifted inside me.

As the party winds down and the kids start to leave, their backpacks bulging with crafts and treats, I find myself lingering. The classroom is a mess of glitter and paper scraps, but there's a cozy, lived-in feel to it that reminds me of my grandmother's house during the holidays.

I tidy up, gathering scraps of wrapping paper and wiping down desks. As I work, my mind wanders back over the past few weeks in Benton Falls. The tree lighting ceremony, volunteering at the book fair, ice skating with Oliver...

Oliver. The thought of him sends a pang through my chest. But it's not the sharp, angry pain of the past two days. It's softer somehow, tinged with regret and a wistfulness I'm not quite ready to examine.

I pick up a crayon drawing left behind on one desk. It shows a stick figure family standing in front of a Christmas tree, surrounded by presents. "My Family" is scrawled across the top in wobbly letters.

Something about the simple drawing catches at my heart. I think about the little girl with the cookie, about how easily she offered kindness to a stranger. I think about Oliver, and how he puts his whole heart into everything he does, whether it's running his store or organizing a toy drive.

And suddenly, with a clarity that takes my breath away, I realize I don't want to go back to who I was before Benton Falls. The thought of returning to my cold, efficient life in Boston, where success is measured in dollars and cents rather than in smiles and acts of kindness, feels impossibly bleak.

I sink into one of the tiny chairs, the crayon drawing still in my hand. The past 48 hours have been miserable, yes, but not because of Benton Falls or Oliver or Christmas. They've been miserable because I've been fighting against the person I've become, trying to force myself back into a mold that no longer fits.

"Oh," I breathe, the realization hitting me like a physical force. "Oh, I've been such an idiot."

"Everything okay in here?" Rebecca's voice from the doorway makes me jump.

I look up at her, feeling dazed. "I... I don't think I can go back to Boston," I say, the words tumbling out before I can stop them.

Rebecca's eyebrows shoot up. "Really? What changed your mind?"

I gesture helplessly around the classroom, at the remnants of the party, at the crayon drawing still clutched in my hand. "All of this. These kids, this town... I've changed, Rebecca. I don't want to be that cold, hard businesswoman anymore. I want to be someone who makes cookies for sad strangers and organizes toy drives and... and believes in the magic of Christmas."

A slow smile spreads across Rebecca's face. "Well," she says softly, "it sounds like you've had quite the epiphany."

I nod, feeling a bit overwhelmed. "I have. But I don't know what to do now. I've messed things up so badly with Oliver..."

Rebecca comes to sit beside me, somehow folding her long legs under the tiny desk. "Chloe," she says gently, "the beautiful thing about Christmas is that it's a time for new beginnings. For forgiveness and hope. It's not too late to make things right."

I look at her, really look at her, and for a moment, I could swear there's something... different about her. A soft glow, maybe, or a depth to her eyes that I've never noticed before. But then I blink, and she's just Rebecca again, smiling at me encouragingly.

"You really think so?" I ask, hating how vulnerable I sound.

Rebecca nods firmly. "I know so. But Chloe, this has to be about more than just Oliver. This has to be about you, about the person you want to be."

Her words resonate deeply within me. She's right, I realize. This isn't just about salvaging a romance or fitting into a small town. It's about becoming the person I've caught glimpses of over the past few weeks—someone kinder, more open, more willing to give of herself.

"You're right," I say, straightening my shoulders. "I need to do this for me. Even if things don't work out with Oliver, even if I end up going back to Boston eventually, I want to be different. Better."

Rebecca's smile is radiant. "That's the spirit. Now, what do you say we finish cleaning up here, and then we can brainstorm about your next steps?"

As we work, chatting and laughing, I feel a lightness in my chest—something akin to anticipation.

By the time we finish, the classroom is spotless, and I have the beginnings of a plan forming in my mind. It's not much – just a few ideas about how to show Oliver I'm sincere, but it's a start.

As we leave the school, the winter sun is already setting, casting long shadows across the snow-covered playground and my plane back to Boston is long gone. The air nips with cold. In the distance, I can hear the faint sound of carolers.

"Thank you, Rebecca," I say as we pause at the

school gates. "For dragging me here today, for everything."

She waves off my thanks with a laugh. "That's what friends are for. Now, go on. You've got some Christmas magic to make happen."

As I walk back towards my grandmother's house, my mind is whirling with plans and possibilities. The twinkling lights of Benton Falls seem brighter somehow, more welcoming. Or maybe it's just that I'm finally seeing them – really seeing them – for the first time.

I pause on the bridge over the Bedford River, looking out at the town spread before me. The courthouse clock chimes the hour, its sound carrying clearly in the still evening air. Somewhere in that sea of lights is Oliver, going about his evening, probably still hurt and angry.

"I'm going to make this right," I whisper into the night. "I'm going to be better. For me, for Oliver, for this town. I promise."

And as I stand there, snow falling gently around me, I feel something I haven't felt in a very long time: hope. Pure, unbridled hope for the future, for the person I'm becoming.

I take a deep breath, letting the cold air fill my lungs. It feels cleansing somehow, like I'm breathing in the spirit of Christmas itself. As I exhale, I let go of the last vestiges of my old self – the cynicism, the fear, the need for control.

Tomorrow is a new day. A day to make amends, to build the life I want, to embrace the magic of Christmas that I've been fighting against for so long.

With a smile on my face and a spring in my step, I head home. Not to Boston, not to my old life, but to the cozy bungalow that's become more of a home to me in a few short weeks than my sleek city apartment ever was.

As I walk, I hum "Silent Night" under my breath. Christmas concerts must be contagious.

Seventeen

CHLOE

I hunker down in my scarf as I make my way towards the Community Christmas Market. Snowflakes dance in the glow of the street lamps, dusting my coat with a fine layer of white. The scent of roasting nuts, sweet treats and deep fried yumminess wafts through the air, growing stronger as I approach the park.

My heart beats a little faster as I round the corner and the market comes into view. It reminds me of a winter wonderland, with wooden stalls adorned with twinkling lights and garlands. The cheerful chatter of shoppers and the distant strains of "Jingle Bells" fill the air.

For a moment, I hesitate at the entrance. Just a few days ago, I was ready to leave all this behind. Now, here I am, willingly diving back into the heart of Benton Falls' Christmas festivities. The irony isn't lost on me.

Taking a deep breath, I step into the market. Immediately, I'm enveloped in warmth and the spirit of the season. Children laugh as they chase each other between the stalls, their parents calling after them with fond exasperation. Couples walk hand in hand, sipping steaming cups of cocoa. The sense of community is palpable, and I feel a pang in my chest as I realize how close I came to giving this up.

"Chloe," a familiar voice calls out. I turn to see Maggie, the owner of Sweet Haven Bakery, waving at me from her stall. The aroma of freshly baked gingerbread and apple pie draws me over.

"Maggie." I greet her with a genuine smile. "Everything smells amazing."

She beams at me; her round face flushed from the cold and the heat of her portable oven. "Why, thank you, dear. I was worried we wouldn't see you again after... well, I heard about you and Oliver."

I feel a twinge of despair at the concern in her voice. "Yeah, but I'm going to fix it," I assure her. "Benton Falls is... it's home now."

The words surprise me as they leave my mouth, but I realize they're true. Somewhere between the toy drive and Christmas concerts, Oliver and this little town have stolen my heart.

Maggie's eyes mist over, and before I know it, I'm enveloped in a warm, flour-dusted hug. "Oh, honey, I'm so glad to hear that. Here, have a gingerbread cookie. On the house."

As I bite into the perfectly spiced cookie, savoring the warmth and sweetness, I spot Mr. Jenkins limping by.

His ankle is still bandaged from his fall at the caroling night.

"Mr. Jenkins," I call out, hurrying over to him. "How are you feeling? Can I help you with anything?"

He looks surprised for a moment, then his face breaks into a kind smile. "Well, if it isn't our city girl. I'm doing much better, thank you. Just here to pick up some gifts for the grandkids."

Without thinking, I offer my arm for support. "Let me help you around. It's the least I can do."

As we make our way through the market, stopping at various stalls, I'm struck by how easily conversation flows. Mr. Jenkins tells me about his grandchildren, about Christmases in Benton Falls when he was a boy, about the year the whole town came together to rebuild the church after a fire. I hang on every word, soaking in the rich history of this place I now call home.

At the toy stall, run by none other than Oliver's right-hand man from the department store, Sam. I smile and say hello, but Sam seems happy to help Mr. Jenkins pick out the perfect gifts—a hand-carved wooden train for little Tommy and a beautiful porcelain doll for Sarah. As I reach for my wallet to pay, Mr. Jenkins stops me.

"Now, now," he says gently. "That's not necessary. Your company and help are gift enough."

I feel a longing in my chest to give to this kind man. "Please," I insist. "Let me do this. Consider it my Christmas gift to you and your grandchildren."

After a moment, he nods, his eyes twinkling. "Well, if

you insist. But you must come over for Christmas dinner then. No arguments."

As we continue our tour of the market, more and more people stop to chat. Mrs. Thompson from the quilting circle asks my opinion on which fabric to choose for her newest project. The school principal thanks me again for helping at the school. Even little Suzie, the girl who gave me the cookie at the school party, runs up to give me a hug, her mother smiling warmly behind her.

With each interaction, I feel the warmth in my chest grow. This, I realize, is what I've been missing all these years. Not just success or achievements, but genuine connections. A sense of belonging.

As we near the reindeer petting zoo, I spot a familiar head of tousled sandy hair. My heart skips a beat.

Oliver.

He's kneeling beside a little boy, helping him feed the reindeer. The sight of him so gentle and patient makes my heart ache with wanting. As if sensing my gaze, he looks up.

For a moment, our eyes lock. I see a flicker of... something in his hazel eyes. Hurt? Longing? Before I can decipher it, he stands abruptly, mumbles something to the zoo attendant, and walks away.

The pain of his rejection is sharp, but it's tempered by the understanding I see in Mr. Jenkins' eyes. "Give him time," the older man says softly.

Sheesh... the whole town must know what happened.

I nod, blinking back tears. "I know. I just... I wish I could make him understand I was only trying to help."

Mr. Jenkins pats my hand. "His pride's taken a hit. He'll come around."

As we complete our circuit of the market, I find myself lost in thought. The twinkling lights, the laughter of children, the sense of warmth and belonging — it all seems bittersweet now. I've found a home here in Benton Falls, but the one person I want to share it with won't even look at me.

"Hey," a cheerful voice breaks through my melancholy. I look up to see Rebecca, her golden hair peeking out from under a festive red hat. "You look a little preoccupied. What are you thinking about?"

"Rebecca," I greet her, managing a small smile. "I was just... thinking."

She links her arm through mine, steering me towards a quiet corner of the market. "About Oliver?" she asks gently.

I nod, not trusting my voice. We stop near the ice skating rink, watching as couples and families glide across the ice, their laughter carried on the cold air.

"I saw him earlier," I admit. "He... he walked away when he saw me."

Rebecca squeezes my arm sympathetically. "Oh, Chloe. I'm so sorry. But you can't give up hope. The course of true love never did run smooth, you know."

I can't help but chuckle at her dramatic delivery. "Shakespeare? Really?"

She grins, unrepentant. "Hey, the classics are classics

for a reason. But seriously, Chloe. Don't lose heart. What you and Oliver have... it's special. It's worth fighting for."

As I look out over the market, taking in the joy and love that seem to radiate from every corner, I feel a renewed sense of determination. "You're right," I say, straightening my shoulders. "I'm not giving up."

Rebecca beams at me, her smile impossibly bright. "That's the spirit. Now, what do you say we go check out the ornament stall? I heard they have some beautiful hand-blown glass ones this year."

As we wander through the market, arm in arm, I truly appreciate the magic of the season for perhaps the first time in my adult life. The way the lights reflect off the snow, creating a warm glow that seems to embrace everything. The sound of carols sung by a group of children, their voices not quite in tune but filled with enthusiasm. The taste of hot mulled cider, spicy and sweet on my tongue.

We stop at a stall selling handmade scarves and gloves. As I run my fingers over the soft wool, an idea begins to form.

"Rebecca," I say slowly, "do you think the market organizers would let me set up a stall? Not to sell anything, but... to give something back to the community?"

Rebecca's eyes light up with interest. "I'm sure they would. What did you have in mind?"

I explain my idea, watching as Rebecca's smile grows wider with each word. By the time I finish, she's practically bouncing with excitement.

"Chloe, that's brilliant," she exclaims. "It's perfect. Oh, we have to make this happen. Come on, let's go talk to the organizers right now."

As we hurry through the market, dodging shoppers and ducking under garlands, I feel a sense of excitement building in my chest. For the first time since my fight with Oliver, I feel truly hopeful. This is my chance to show Benton Falls—to show Oliver—who I really am. Who I want to be.

We find the market coordinator, Mrs. Clausen, near the hot chocolate stand. She listens to my proposal with growing interest, her eyes twinkling.

"Well, Chloe," she says when I finish, "I think that's a wonderful idea. We'd be delighted to have you join us. How soon can you be ready?"

I glance at Rebecca, who gives me an encouraging nod. "Tomorrow," I say firmly. "I can be ready by tomorrow."

As we leave Mrs. Clausen to make the necessary arrangements, Rebecca turns to me with a grin. "Well, looks like we've got a busy night ahead of us. Ready to spread some Christmas cheer, Benton Falls style?"

I laugh, feeling lighter than I have in days. "Ready as I'll ever be. Let's do this."

We spend the rest of the evening planning and preparing, fueled by excitement and more than a little Christmas magic. As the night wears on and our plans take shape, I find myself filled with a sense of purpose I've never felt before. This isn't about business strategies or profit margins. It's about giving back, about being part of something bigger than myself.

As I finally crawl into bed in the early hours of the morning, exhausted but exhilarated, I send up a silent prayer of thanks. For Rebecca's friendship, for the warmth of this community, for the chance to become the person I want to be.

Eighteen

CHLOE

The next morning dawns bright and cold, the sun glinting off the fresh snow that fell overnight. I'm up with the birds, too excited and nervous to sleep any longer. As I sip my coffee, looking out at the winter wonderland that is Benton Falls, I feel a mix of anticipation and trepidation.

Today's the day. The day I show this town—and hopefully, Oliver — that I'm here to stay. That I understand now what it means to be part of a community, to give without expectation of return.

Rebecca arrives just as I'm finishing my second cup of coffee, her arms laden with supplies. Her enthusiasm is infectious, and soon we're both caught up in a flurry of activity, packing up everything we need for our surprise at the market.

As we make our way to the park, the streets are still quiet. Most of the town is still asleep. But there's a sense of anticipation in the air, as if Benton Falls itself is holding its breath, waiting to see what the day will bring.

We set up our stall in record time, hanging the banner I stayed up half the night painting: "Chloe's Christmas Wish." The table is laden with an assortment of items - gift cards, handmade crafts, toys, and more - all waiting to be given away.

As the market comes to life around us, people gather, curious about the new stall. I take a deep breath, steeling myself for what's to come.

"Good morning, everyone," I say, my voice only slightly shaky. "I'm Chloe Anderson, and I'm here today to grant Christmas wishes. If there's something you need this holiday season—a gift you can't afford, a repair you've been putting off, or even just a helping hand—I want to help make it happen."

For a moment, there's silence. Then, slowly, people step forward. An elderly woman who needs her roof fixed before winter truly sets in. A young mother who can't afford a Christmas gift for her son. A teenager who dreams of taking art classes but can't spare the money.

One by one, I listen to their stories, their wishes, their hopes. And one by one, I do my best to make those wishes come true. Gift cards are distributed, promises of services are made, and slowly, the pile on the table dwindles as the smiles in the crowd grow.

As the day progresses, I notice something strange happening. Little miracles seem to occur all around me, things I can't quite explain.

When Mrs. Thompson wishes for a specific type of

rare wool for her quilting project, a vendor I've never seen before appears out of nowhere with exactly what she needs. When little Timmy's mother mentions he's always wanted to learn to ice skate but can't afford lessons, the skating rink manager suddenly shows up, offering free lessons for underprivileged kids.

At first, I chalk it up to the spirit of the season and the generosity of the Benton Falls community. But as these coincidences pile up, I can't shake the feeling that something more is at play.

I glance at Rebecca, who's been by my side all day, helping to organize and manage the wish-granting. She has an impish grin on her face, her eyes twinkling with barely contained mischief. Every time one of these little miracles occurs, her smile grows wider.

During a lull in the crowd, I pull her aside. "Rebecca," I whisper, "what's going on? How are all these perfect solutions just... appearing out of thin air?"

She blinks at me innocently, but I can see the laughter dancing in her eyes. "Why, whatever do you mean, Chloe? It's Christmas. Miracles happen, don't they?"

I narrow my eyes at her. "Rebecca, I'm serious. It's like... it's like magic or something. Wait a minute..." I trail off, a ridiculous thought forming in my mind. "Are you some kind of... Christmas fairy or something?"

Rebecca bursts out laughing, the sound like tinkling bells. "A Christmas fairy? Oh, Chloe, you have quite the imagination." She winks at me. "Let's just say I have some... connections. And leave it at that, shall we?"

Before I can press her further, another person approaches the stall with a wish, and we're swept back into the whirlwind of giving. But I can't shake the feeling that there's more to Rebecca than meets the eye.

Throughout the rest of the day, I keep catching glimpses of Rebecca whispering to thin air, or making subtle gestures when she thinks I'm not looking. And each time, another small miracle occurs. A lost heirloom is found. A broken appliance mysteriously starts working again. A long-lost friend suddenly appears in town for a surprise visit.

It's baffling and wonderful, and just a little terrifying. But as I watch the joy spreading through the market, see the smiles on people's faces and the tears of happiness in their eyes, I decide maybe it doesn't matter how these miracles are happening. What matters is that they are happening, and that they're bringing light and hope to so many people.

As the sun sets and we start packing up the stall, I pull Rebecca into a hug. "I don't know how you did it," I murmur, "but thank you. This day... it's been magical."

Rebecca hugs me back tightly. "Oh, Chloe," she says, her voice warm with affection, "the magic was always there. In you, in this town, in the spirit of giving. I just... gave it a little nudge."

I pull back, studying her face. For a moment, I could swear I see a faint glow around her, like starlight caught in her golden hair. But then I blink, and she's just Rebecca again, smiling at me with that mischievous twinkle in her eye.

"Now," she says briskly, "let's finish cleaning up. I have a feeling there's one more miracle waiting to happen today."

And sure enough, as we're putting the last of the boxes away, I hear footsteps approaching. I turn, and my breath catches in my throat. Oliver.

He stops a few feet away, his hands shoved in his pockets, looking uncertain. "Chloe," he says softly. "I... what you did today. It was incredible."

Hope blooms in my chest, fragile but undeniable. "Oliver, I—"

He holds up a hand, stopping me. "I'm not saying everything's okay. We still have a lot to talk about. But... I'd like to hear what you have to say. Maybe over coffee? Tomorrow?"

I nod, not trusting my voice. Oliver gives me a small smile—not the full, warm grin I've grown to love, but a start. A promise of possibility.

As he walks away, I turn back to the boxes, my heart lighter than it's been in days. In that moment, I swear I can feel the spirit of the season all around me.

Tomorrow is another day. Another chance to make things right, to continue becoming the person I want to be. The journey isn't over yet.

After all, 'tis the season for miracles.

Nineteen

REBECCA

The last of the twinkling lights flicker out as I stand in the now-deserted Benton Falls Christmas Market. The bustling energy of the day has faded, leaving behind a peaceful quiet broken only by the soft crunch of snow beneath my feet. Sugar and spice linger in the air, a sweet reminder of the day's festivities.

I close my eyes, replaying the events of the day in my mind. Chloe's radiant smile as she granted wish after wish at her "Chloe's Christmas Wish" stall. The joy on people's faces as little miracles unfolded around them. And finally, the tentative hope in both Chloe and Oliver's eyes as they briefly talked—I'm optimistic.

A sense of accomplishment washes over me, warm and comforting, like a cozy blanket on a cold winter's night. When I open my eyes, a flicker of light catches my eye.

"Quite a day, wasn't it?" Henry's warm voice reaches

my ears as he materializes beside me, his silver hair slightly disheveled as always.

I nod, unable to keep the smile off my face. "It was magical, Henry. I've never felt anything like it."

Henry chuckles, the sound reminding me of jingle bells. "Oh?"

His question makes me pause. I take a moment to really consider how I've changed since starting this assignment.

"I feel... different," I say slowly. "When I started, all I cared about was earning my wings. I thought I knew everything, that I was somehow above it all. But now..."

"Now?" Henry prompts gently.

I gesture towards the empty market stalls around us. "Now I understand what it really means to be a guardian angel. It's not about power or prestige. It's about love, about service, about helping people find the light within themselves."

Henry's smile is warm and proud. "That, my dear, is the most important lesson any angel can learn. And you've learned it beautifully."

As we stand there in the quiet of the night, I can't help but think back on all the little miracles that have led us to this point. The 'blessing hotline' and the boots, the Miracle Card helping Chloe grant Christmas wishes. But it's Chloe herself who's done the real work, who's opened her heart to the spirit of Christmas and the joy of giving.

"I think Chloe was starting to suspect I'm not quite what I seem," I say to Henry, a mischievous grin spreading across my face. "She asked me earlier if I was some kind of Christmas fairy."

Henry lets out a hearty laugh. "Well, you're not too far off, are you? Though I daresay you're a bit more powerful than a fairy."

I giggle, the sound like tinkling bells on Christmas Eve. "Don't let the fairies hear you say that. They can be quite touchy about their powers."

As our laughter subsides, I find my thoughts drifting to Chloe and Oliver. "Do you think they'll work things out?" I ask Henry, unable to keep the worry from my voice.

Henry's expression turns thoughtful. "That, my dear, is up to them."

I nod, understanding the truth of his words. It's a lesson I've learned well over the course of this assignment. We can't force people to make the right choices; we can only help light the way and hope they choose to follow.

"But you know what, Henry?" I say, feeling a sense of peace settle over me. "Whatever happens between Chloe and Oliver, I know Chloe will be okay. She's found something here in Benton Falls that goes beyond romantic love. She's found herself, her purpose, her place in the world."

Henry nods approvingly. "You've come a long way, Rebecca. You understand now that our job isn't just about making people happy in the moment. It's about helping them grow, helping them become the best versions of themselves."

As we walk through the deserted market, our footsteps leaving trails in the fresh snow, I reflect on all I've learned during my time on Earth.

"When I first started this assignment," I look at Henry. "I thought being a guardian angel was all about big, dramatic interventions. Saving people from physical danger, performing obvious miracles, that sort of thing."

Henry nods encouragingly, prompting me to continue.

"But now I understand that it's the small things that often make the biggest difference. A kind word at the right moment, a small act of generosity, creating opportunities for people to discover their own strength and goodness. It's about guiding, not controlling. About love, not power."

Henry's smile is radiant. "You've learned well, Rebecca. Those are lessons that many angels take centuries to truly understand."

As we reach the edge of the park, I feel the familiar tingle of celestial energy, signaling it's time to return to the heavenly realm. But I hesitate, looking back at the town of Benton Falls, its windows glowing warmly in the night.

"It's time to go, Rebecca," Henry says gently. "We've done all we can here."

I nod, knowing he's right, but finding it hard to tear my eyes away from the town that's taught me so much. "Will they be okay?" I can't help but ask one last time.

Henry's smile is knowing. "They have all the tools they need to find their way. The rest is up to them."

With one last look at Benton Falls, I close my eyes and let the familiar sensation of celestial teleportation wash over me. When I open them again, I'm standing in the ethereal glow of the heavenly realm, the earthly scents and sounds of Benton Falls replaced by the indescribable beauty of paradise.

Henry waves as he walks towards the gardens and I turn toward my apartment. I think I've earned my wings, but I'm not done. I must go back to Benton Falls at least one more time. To say my goodbyes to Chloe—even if she doesn't know it's goodbye—and even though it's not my assignment, if there is anything I can do to help Chloe and Oliver come back to each other, I will.

Because now I understand - being a guardian angel is a lot like being a good friend.

Twenty

CHLOE

T he bell above the door of Sweet Haven Bakery & Café jingles merrily as I step inside, shaking snow from my boots. The warm aroma of freshly baked cinnamon rolls and brewing coffee envelops me, instantly melting away the chill from outside. Christmas carols play softly in the background, mingling with the cheerful chatter of patrons.

My eyes scan the cozy interior, taking in the rustic wooden beams overhead and the exposed brick walls adorned with vintage bakery signs. The morning sunlight streams through the large bay windows, casting a golden glow over everything. It feels like stepping into a Christmas card come to life.

Then I spot him. Oliver is seated at a corner table, his sandy hair slightly tousled, a steaming mug cradled in his hands. My heart does a little flip at the sight of him. Taking a deep breath to steady my nerves, I make my way over.

"Hi," I say softly as I approach the table.

Oliver looks up, his hazel eyes warming as they meet mine. "Chloe," he says, standing up. "I'm glad you came."

For a moment, we just stand there, an awkward tension hanging between us. Then Oliver gestures to the chair across from him. "Please, sit. I got you a latte. I hope that's okay."

I slide into the seat, wrapping my cold fingers around the warm mug. "It's perfect, thank you."

We sit in silence for a few seconds, both seemingly unsure of where to start. The weight of all that's happened, all that needs to be said, feels almost tangible between us.

Before Oliver can speak, I blurt out, "I want to help with the toy drive."

Oliver blinks, clearly taken aback. "What?"

I take a deep breath, pushing on. "The toy drive. I want to help finish it up, help deliver the toys... if you'll still have me, that is."

I watch Oliver's face carefully, trying to gauge his reaction. To my dismay, he seems uneasy, his brow furrowing slightly. My heart sinks. He doesn't want me involved in any part of his life.

"Chloe, I—" he begins, but I cut him off, the words tumbling out in a rush.

"I'm sorry, Oliver. I'm so sorry about everything. But I want you to know, even if I didn't know you, even if I had just wandered into Benton Falls by chance, I would want to invest in a place like Hanks' Department Store.

It's special, Oliver. You've created something truly inspiring there."

To my surprise, Oliver reaches across the table and takes my hand. The warmth of his touch sends a shiver through me that has nothing to do with the cold outside.

"Chloe," he says softly, his eyes filled with a mix of emotions I can't quite decipher. "I'm the one who should be apologizing. I was prideful and short-sighted. Your help... your investment... I'm incredibly grateful for it."

I feel tears pricking at the corners of my eyes, hope blooming in my chest. "Really?"

Oliver nods, a rueful smile playing at his lips. "Really. In fact, this entire experience has made me realize something. I need to change. I need to accept help, to incorporate new ideas on how to run the store. I've been so focused on preserving the past that I've been resistant to embracing the future. And the truth is... I need you, Chloe."

His words send a warmth spreading through me that has nothing to do with the latte I'm drinking. "Oliver, I —" I start, but then pause, realizing this is the perfect moment to share my news. "Actually, I have something to tell you. I'm... well, I'm currently unemployed. I resigned from my position in Boston."

Oliver's eyebrows shoot up in surprise. "You did? But I thought... I mean, your career seemed so important to you."

I nod, a small smile playing at my lips. "It was. But I've realized there are more important things in life than corner offices and corporate success. Things like community, connection... love."

The last word hangs in the air between us, loaded with meaning. Oliver's eyes soften, a smile spreading across his face that makes my heart skip a beat.

"Well," he says, a hint of mischief in his voice, "in that case, how would you like a job?"

I blink, surprised. "A job?"

Oliver nods, his eyes twinkling. "Just for the day to start with. You see, it's Christmas Eve Eve, and I could really use some extra help at the store. In fact," he glances at his watch, "I should get back there now to help Sam out."

For a moment, I'm speechless. Then a laugh bubbles up from deep inside me, joyous and free. "Yes," I say, grinning from ear to ear. "Yes, I'd love a job."

Oliver stands, extending his hand to me. "Well then, Ms. Anderson, shall we head to work?"

As I take his hand, I'm struck by how right this feels. How perfectly I fit into this life, this town, this moment. "Lead the way, Mr. Hanks."

We step out of the cafe into the frosty winter air, snowflakes dancing around us. The town square is a hive of activity, people rushing about with last-minute Christmas preparations. But amid the hustle and bustle, there's a sense of joy, of community, that permeates everything.

As we walk towards Hanks' Department Store, hand in hand, I'm overwhelmed by a wave of emotion. Gratitude for this second chance with Oliver. Love for this town and its people who have welcomed me so warmly. And a deep, abiding joy at the transformation I've undergone.

"Oliver," I say, stopping in the middle of the square. He turns to me, a question in his eyes. "I just... I need you to know how much this all means to me. You, this town, the spirit of Christmas that I've found here. It's transformed me in ways I never thought possible."

Oliver's eyes soften, and he reaches up to brush a snowflake from my cheek. "Chloe," he says softly, "you've transformed this town too. The way you threw yourself into helping others, the joy you've brought to so many people... you embody the true spirit of Christmas."

His words warm me from the inside out. Standing here in the gently falling snow, the sounds of carols and laughter drifting around us, I feel a sense of peace and rightness that I've never experienced before.

"I love you, Oliver," I say, the words coming easily, naturally. "And I love Benton Falls. I want to be part of this community, to continue spreading joy and helping others. I think... I think I've finally found my true purpose."

Oliver's smile is radiant as he pulls me close. "I love you too, Chloe," he murmurs. "And I'm so glad you've found your home here."

As Oliver leans in, the world around us seems to slow down. I catch the faint scent of his cologne mingling with the brisk winter air and a hint of cinnamon from the bakery nearby. His hazel eyes hold mine for a moment before fluttering closed.

Our lips meet in a tender kiss, soft and warm against the cool December air. I taste a hint of peppermint on his breath. The gentle pressure of his lips on mine sends a tingling sensation through my body, from the top of my head to the tips of my toes.

As we kiss, I hear the town clock chime the hour. The deep, resonant tones seem to reverberate through me, marking not just the time, but the start of a new chapter in my life. The sound mingles with the soft rustle of snowflakes falling around us and the distant echoes of Christmas carols from a nearby shop.

Oliver's arms encircle me, strong and secure. I feel the rough wool of his coat beneath my fingertips as I rest my hands on his chest, the steady beat of his heart a comforting rhythm against my palm. The warmth of his embrace contrasts deliciously with the cold snowflakes melting on my cheeks.

As we slowly part, my eyes flutter open to see Oliver's face, his expression one of pure joy and love. The world comes back into focus around us—the twinkling lights, the gently falling snow, the bustling town square—but everything seems brighter, more vivid than before.

This kiss, this moment, has awakened all my senses, making me feel more alive than I've ever felt. It's as if I'm experiencing the magic of Christmas, of love, of Benton Falls, all at once, with every fiber of my being.

We break apart, both a little breathless, grins on our faces. "Come on," Oliver says, tugging gently on my hand. "We've got a store to run and some Christmas magic to make."

Twenty-One

CHLOE

As we walk towards Hanks' Department Store, I can't help but marvel at how much has changed in such a short time. Just a few weeks ago, I was a cold, career-driven woman who saw Christmas as nothing more than an inconvenience. Now, here I am, heart full of love, ready to dive into the chaos of a small-town Christmas Eve Eve.

The store is a whirlwind of activity when we arrive. Customers browse the aisles, last-minute shoppers frantically search for the perfect gifts, and in the midst of it all, Sam mans the register with a harried but cheerful expression.

"Oh, thank goodness you're here," he says as we enter, relief evident in his voice. Then he spots me and his eyebrows shoot up. "Chloe? Are you...?"

"She's here to help," Oliver explains, a proud smile on his face. "Our newest employee, at least for today."

Sam's face breaks into a wide grin. "Well, thank the

Christmas angels for that. Chloe, think you can handle gift wrapping? Rebecca's restocking shelves as we speak."

I nod, rolling up my sleeves and smile as Rebecca comes wandering from the back room, her arms full of boxes. "Point me to the paper and ribbons, Sam. I'm ready to spread some Christmas cheer."

For the next few hours, I lose myself in a flurry of colorful paper, shiny ribbons, and the joy of helping people find the perfect finishing touch for their gifts. I chat with customers, learning about their holiday traditions, the loved ones they're shopping for, the stories behind each carefully chosen present.

As I tie a bow on a gift for a little girl's first Christmas, I catch sight of Oliver across the store. He's kneeling beside an older gentleman, patiently explaining the features of a new coffeemaker. The care and attention he gives to each customer, the genuine warmth in his interactions, make my heart swell with love and pride.

Rebecca gives me an approving nod and winks when she sees me talking to Oliver. I smile, feeling so blessed to have a friend like Rebecca. Somehow, she's always in the right place at the right time.

Throughout the day, I witness countless small acts of kindness and generosity. A young boy emptying his piggy bank to buy a scarf for his mother. A woman purchasing an extra toy to donate to the toy drive. Oliver slipping a free ornament into the bag of a customer who's had a tough year.

These moments, these little miracles of human kindness, fill me with a joy so profound it's almost overwhelming. This, I realize, is what Christmas is truly about. Not the presents or the decorations, but the love we share, the connections we forge, the light we bring to each other's lives.

As the day wears on and the crowd in the store begins to thin, I find myself by the Christmas tree in the corner. It's a magnificent thing, towering nearly to the ceiling, adorned with an eclectic mix of ornaments that I now know has been donated by town residents over the years.

"What's going on in that pretty head of yours?" Oliver's voice breaks through my reverie. I turn to find him standing beside me, a soft smile on his face.

"I was just thinking about how beautiful this tree is," I say, gesturing to the twinkling lights and glittering ornaments. "Each piece has a story, a memory attached to it. It's like a physical representation of the community spirit in Benton Falls."

Oliver nods, his eyes twinkling. "That's exactly what it is. And now," he reaches into his pocket and pulls out a small, wrapped package, "it's time to add your story to the tree."

I unwrap the package with trembling fingers to reveal a delicate glass ornament. It's a miniature version of Oliver's department store, complete with tiny Christmas lights and a minuscule version of the two of us standing out front.

"Oliver," I breathe, tears pricking at my eyes. "It's beautiful."

He takes the ornament gently from my hands and hangs it on a prominent branch of the tree. "There," he says softly. "Now you're officially part of Benton Falls history."

I lean into him, overcome with emotion. "Thank you," I whisper. "For everything. For showing me what Christmas is really about, for helping me find my place in this world."

Oliver wraps his arm around me, pulling me close. "Thank you for bringing new life to this town, and to me," he says. "You've reminded all of us of the magic of Christmas, of the joy of giving and the power of love."

As we stand there, bathed in the soft glow of the Christmas lights, I feel a deep sense of peace and fulfillment wash over me. I've found my purpose, my home, my heart. And it's all wrapped up in this quaint little town and the wonderful man beside me.

The sound of the door chime breaks the moment, and we turn to see Sam ushering in a group of carolers. "Hope you don't mind," he calls out to us. "They wanted to thank the store for supporting the community choir this year."

As the first notes of "Silent Night" fill the air, customers and staff alike gather around the tree. Oliver takes my hand, and we join the impromptu audience. Looking around at the faces lit by candlelight and Christmas lights, I see the same joy and wonder I feel reflected at me.

In this moment, surrounded by the warmth of community and the spirit of the season, I know without a doubt that this is where I belong. Benton Falls isn't just a town I stumbled into by chance; it's the home I've been searching for all my life.

As the carolers finish their song and the applause dies down, Oliver turns to me with a mischievous glint in his eye. "So, Ms. Anderson," he says, loud enough for everyone to hear, "what do you say? Ready to make this job permanent? Benton Falls could use someone with your business sense and generous heart."

The store falls silent, all eyes on me. But for once, I don't feel the pressure of expectations or the weight of others' judgment. Instead, I feel the warm support of a community that has accepted me as one of their own.

"Mr. Hanks," I reply, my voice ringing clear and confident, "I would be honored to accept a permanent position at Hanks' Department Store. On one condition."

Oliver raises an eyebrow, a smile playing at his lips. "And what condition would that be?"

I grin, joy bubbling up inside me. "That the position comes with the perk of being able to kiss the boss whenever I want."

The store erupts in cheers and laughter as Oliver pulls me into his arms. "I think that can be arranged," he murmurs before capturing my lips in a kiss that promises a lifetime of love and happiness.

As we break apart, breathless and grinning, I'm struck by how perfectly everything has fallen into place. The store, with its blend of tradition and innovation, is a reflection of the future Oliver and I will build together.

A future that honors the past while embracing new possibilities.

The rest of the evening passes in a blur of laughter, music, and the warm glow of Christmas lights. Rebecca wishes us a Merry Christmas before she leaves. As we finally close up the store, the last customer ushered out with wishes for a joyous holiday, I feel a sense of excited anticipation for what the future holds.

Oliver and I walk hand in hand through the quiet streets of Benton Falls, the fresh snow crunching beneath our feet. The town is peaceful now, houses glowing with warm light, the occasional sound of laughter or the faint strains of a Christmas movie drifting through the night air.

We pause at the end of the street, looking out at the town spread before us. The Christmas lights reflect off the blanket of snow, creating a magical, shimmering effect.

"You know," I say softly, leaning into Oliver's warmth, "a month ago, if someone had told me I'd be standing here, in love with a small-town shopkeeper and ready to give up my big city career, I would have thought they were crazy."

Oliver chuckles, the sound rumbling through his chest. "And if someone had told me that a big city CEO would sweep into town and steal my heart while saving my business, I wouldn't have believed them either."

I turn to face him, taking both his hands in mine. "Thank you, Oliver. For showing me what really matters in life. For helping me rediscover the magic of Christmas and the joy of giving."

Oliver's eyes shine with love as he gazes down at me. "Thank you, Chloe, for bringing new life to this town and to me. For reminding us all of the true spirit of Christmas."

As we stand there on the bridge, snow gently falling around us, I'm filled with a sense of wonder and gratitude. For the journey that brought me here, for the love I've found, for the community that's welcomed me with open arms.

As the town clock chimes midnight, marking the start of Christmas Eve, Oliver pulls me close. "Merry Christmas, Chloe," he whispers.

"Merry Christmas, Oliver," I reply, my heart full to bursting with love and joy.

And as we seal the moment with a kiss, I silently thank whatever twist of fate brought me to this magical little town. Because here in Benton Falls, I've not only found the true meaning of Christmas, but I've also found myself, my home, and a love that will last a lifetime.

The spirit of giving, I realize, isn't just about presents or grand gestures. It's about opening your heart, sharing your joy, and spreading love wherever you go. And that's a lesson I'll carry with me, not just at Christmas, but every day of the year.

Epilogue

REBECCA

The soft, golden glow of celestial light pulses gently around me as I stand before the grand lectern in the heavenly hall. The cool marble floor beneath my feet ground me, a stark contrast to the sense of vastness that stretches above and around me. The air itself seems to shimmer with divine energy, carrying the faint scent of stardust and eternity.

I take a deep breath, my gaze falling on Henry and the Archangel Saint Nicholas seated in the front row. Their presence both comforts and intimidates me. Henry's kind blue eyes twinkle with encouragement, while Saint Nicholas's piercing gaze seems to look right through me, as if he can see every thought and emotion swirling within my soul.

The weight of the moment settles upon me. This is it. My dissertation. The culmination of my journey as a guardian angel in training. Everything I've learned, everything I've experienced, has led to this moment.

I clear my throat; the sound echoing in the vast space. "Esteemed Archangel Saint Nicholas, beloved mentor Henry, I stand before you today to present my dissertation on my first assignment as a guardian angel in training."

As I begin to speak, I feel a warmth spreading through me. It's not the burning ambition I used to feel, the desperate need to prove myself and earn status. Instead, it's a gentle glow of love, compassion, and understanding. It's the spirit of Christmas, the essence of what it means to be a guardian angel, alive within me.

"My assignment was Chloe Anderson," I continue, my voice growing stronger. "A successful businesswoman who had lost touch with the true meaning of Christmas, of family, of love itself."

As I speak, I find myself transported back to those first days in Benton Falls. The crisp winter air, the twinkling lights reflected in the snow, the sound of carols drifting on the breeze. I can almost smell the rich aroma of Maggie's gingerbread cookies, taste the warmth of her hot chocolate on my tongue.

"When I first met Chloe," I say, "I saw only a cold, ambitious woman who cared for nothing but success and money. But as I got to know her, as I watched her interact with the people of Benton Falls, I saw beneath the surface."

I pause, remembering the moment I first saw Chloe's walls begin to crumble. The look in her eyes when she helped a child pick out a gift for their mother. The way her voice softened when she spoke of her grandmother.

"I learned that Chloe's drive for success came from a place of deep-seated fear and insecurity. Her childhood experiences of poverty and loss had left her believing that financial success was the only path to happiness and security."

As I speak, I notice a shift in the hall's atmosphere. The air seems to shimmer with increased intensity, and I swear I can smell the faint scent of pine and cinnamon. It's as if Benton Falls itself is materializing around us, bringing a touch of earthly Christmas magic to this celestial realm.

"My task was not just to help Chloe rediscover the spirit of Christmas," I continue, "but to help her heal the wounds of her past by opening her heart to love and connection."

I go on to describe the various challenges and triumphs of my assignment. The community caroling night where Chloe first softened. The Christmas market where she granted wishes and spread joy. The moment she decided to anonymously donate to save Oliver's store.

As I speak, I can feel the emotions of those moments washing over me once again. The joy, the frustration, the hope, the love. I realize now that it wasn't just Chloe who was transformed by this experience. I, too, have been fundamentally changed.

"But the most important lesson I learned," I say, my voice filled with emotion, "is that being a guardian angel isn't about grand gestures or miraculous interventions. It's about the small moments of kindness, the gentle nudges in the right direction, the quiet presence in times of need."

I look directly at Henry as I say this, seeing the pride shining in his eyes. He nods encouragingly, urging me to continue.

"I learned that genuine change comes not from external forces, but from within. My role was not to force Chloe to change, but to create opportunities for her to discover her own capacity for love and generosity."

As I continue my dissertation, I reflect on my journey. How I started this assignment focused only on earning my wings, on proving myself. How, through helping Chloe, I discovered my own capacity for empathy and selfless love.

"In the end," I say, my voice ringing clear and strong through the hall, "Chloe not only rediscovered the spirit of Christmas, but she also found love, purpose, and a true sense of belonging. She transformed from a woman who measured her worth in dollars and cents to one who finds joy in giving, in connection, in being part of a community."

I pause, taking a deep breath before delivering my conclusion. "But perhaps the most profound transformation was my own. Through guiding Chloe, I learned the true meaning of being a guardian angel. It's not about power or prestige. It's about love, service, and the joy of helping others find the light within themselves."

As I finish speaking, a hush falls over the hall. The celestial light seems to pulse more intensely, and I swear I can hear the faint echo of Christmas bells in the distance.

Saint Nicholas leans forward, his piercing blue eyes fixed on me. "Thank you, Rebecca, for your heartfelt dissertation. Before we proceed, do you have any final thoughts to share?"

I nod, surprised to feel tears pricking at my eyes. "Yes." I collect myself. "I want to express my profound gratitude. To Henry, for his patient guidance and wisdom. To Chloe, for teaching me more about love and resilience than I ever could have imagined. And to the divine power that gave me this opportunity to grow and serve."

As I speak these words, I feel a warmth spreading through me, starting in my heart and radiating outward. It's a feeling of pure love and joy, more powerful than anything I've ever experienced.

Saint Nicholas smiles, a sight so beautiful it nearly takes my breath away. "Rebecca," he says, his voice like the peal of golden bells, "you have showed remarkable growth and understanding. Your journey from a self-centered weather forecaster to a compassionate guardian angel is truly commendable."

I hold my breath, hardly daring to hope.

"It is with great pleasure," Saint Nicholas continues, "that I bestow upon you your wings. May you continue to bring light and love to those in need, and may your service be a beacon of hope in the world."

As he speaks these words, Henry rings a bell. I feel a tingling sensation between my shoulder blades. A soft glow wraps around me, and I gasp as I feel my newly manifested wings unfurling behind me. They're not heavy or awkward, but an extension of my being.

Overwhelmed with emotion, I turn to Henry, who is beaming with pride. "Oh, Rebecca," he says, pulling me into a warm embrace. "I'm so proud of you. You understand now, don't you? The wings aren't the goal. The service, the love, the growth—that's what being a guardian angel is all about."

I nod, feeling tears of joy stream down my face. "I understand. And I'm so grateful for this journey."

As the ceremony concludes and I prepare to embark on my next assignment, I find my thoughts drifting back to Benton Falls. To Chloe and Oliver, to the warmth of the community and to the spirit of giving and love—the true essence of Christmas, that I was privileged to be a part of.

I may have earned my wings, but I've gained something far more valuable - a true understanding of what it means to be a guardian angel.

Continue reading for a glimpse into Angel Institute Book 5: *Matthew.*

Spend more time with angels in training this Christmas!

Angel Institute Book 5

JOHN

I sit nervously in my chair, my fingers absently adjusting the colorful socks that peek out from beneath my celestial robes. Today's socks have books, freshly sharpened pencils, and A+s on them. We're getting our final assignments, and they just feel right.

As always, I've come prepared - my notebook is open before me, filled with neatly written lists and carefully drawn flowcharts. Planning has always been my forte, a way to make sense of the unpredictable. I find comfort in structure and organization. God loves order. I see it everywhere in heaven and on earth. My penchant for creating systems is one of the ways I know I am His.

Around me, nine other angels-in-training await their assignments. We've been together for a while now, holding study sessions and dreaming about our wings. I'm one of the best study buddies around because I've meticulously documented every lesson. You need notes? I have them.

Henry, our mentor and instructor, stands at the front of the room, his majestic wings folded behind him. He told us the story of getting his wings on the first day of class. It's such an inspiring story—one that gave us all hope that we, too, can become first-class angels. I want to ease people's burdens and sorrows. There's so much to be happy about if only one plans for it properly.

As Henry begins his speech, I ready my pen, prepared to jot down every crucial detail of our final assignment. "Welcome, my dear trainees," he says, his voice calm and reassuring. "Today is a big day. Each of you will receive a letter with your final assignment on Earth. I should tell you that you'll be going down during the Christmas season."

My mind immediately starts racing, thinking of all the potential scenarios I might encounter and the strategies I might need to employ. I start a new list in my notebook: "Christmas Spirit Boosters. 1. Decorating. 2. Music. 3. Sermons. 4. Nativity scenes. 5. Service. ..."

When Henry mentions the possibility of failure, I feel a knot forming in my stomach and leave off finishing my list. I raise my hand. "Is failure... possible?"

Henry assures me that it is possible but unlikely. I add a new item to my list: "6. Focus on the good. 7. Work in faith."

He walks down the aisles, handing out our letters.

My hands tremble slightly as I take the thick envelope. I open it carefully, ready to start mapping out my approach. It's pretty straightforward and yet complex.

I immediately flip to a new page in my notebook,

titling it "Operation: Connect Matthew to his Family." My mind is already racing. *Step 1. Find out who his family is. Step 2. Find out why they aren't together. Step 3. Fix it.*

Sounds simple. Looks easy enough on paper.

I leave the classroom, clutching my notebook tightly to my chest, a comforting weight filled with lists, plans, and hopes.

"Okay, John," I mutter to myself, wiggling my toes. "Time to bring some Christmas cheer to Earth."

To continue reading, grab book 5 in The Angel Institute Christmas Series.

The angels in training are waiting for you!
Enjoy all the Christmas stories that fill your heart with holiday joy.

Acknowledgments

Writing a book is never a solitary endeavor, and we are profoundly grateful for the incredible team of individuals who have supported us throughout this journey.

First and foremost, we want to express our heartfelt thanks to our amazing beta readers: Rolayne, Marissa, and Renee. Your keen insights, thoughtful feedback, and unwavering enthusiasm have been invaluable. You truly are the best beta readers we could have hoped for, and this series is better because of your contributions.

A special thank you goes to Richard for his meticulous consistency read. Your eagle eye for detail and ability to catch those elusive inconsistencies that somehow slip through have been instrumental in polishing our work to a shine.

We are deeply appreciative of Shaylee for her unwavering support and for helping us launch the Angels Unscripted podcast. Your creativity and dedication have opened up new avenues for us to connect with our readers and share the world of the Angel Institute.

To our wonderful reviewers, we cannot thank you enough. Your thoughtful words and enthusiasm for our books have been a constant source of motivation. Your efforts in spreading the word about the Angel Institute series have been crucial in helping us reach new readers. We are truly grateful for your support and advocacy.

Lastly, to our readers – thank you for embarking on this heavenly adventure with us. Your love for our characters and stories makes all the late nights and rewrites worthwhile.

This series is a labor of love, made possible by the collective efforts of many. We are blessed to have such an incredible community surrounding us, and we thank you all from the bottom of our hearts.

Book Club Questions

Hello, fellow readers!

We're excited you've chosen *Angel Institute: Your Assignment: Chloe* for your book club. Now that you've journeyed through Chloe's struggles as she learns about the Spirit of Giving at Christmas, it's time to dive deeper into the heart of the story.

These questions are designed to get you thinking about the bigger picture—the themes, character arcs, and those "aha!" moments that made the story come alive.

Whether you're pondering the challenges faced by our guardian angels in training or dissecting the complexities of human nature, we hope these questions will enrich your reading experience and lead to some enlightening discussions.

So grab your favorite beverage, settle in with your book club, and let's explore the heavenly and earthly realms of Angel Institute together. Happy discussing!

- How does the author portray the theme of "the spirit of Christmas"? What does this mean to different characters in the book?
- Compare and contrast Chloe's life in the city with her experiences in Benton Falls. What does this reveal about her character?
- Discuss the relationship between Chloe and Oliver. How does it develop, and what obstacles do they face?
- How does Rebecca's character grow throughout the story? How does her understanding of being a guardian angel change?
- What role does community play in the novel? How does it impact Chloe's transformation?
- Discuss the symbolism of Hanks' Department Store. What does it represent to Oliver, Chloe, and the town?
- How does the author use holiday traditions and events to advance the plot and develop characters?
- What does Chloe's anonymous donation to save Oliver's store reveal about her character? Why does it initially cause conflict?
- How does the book explore the theme of vulnerability? Which characters struggle with this, and how do they overcome it?
- Discuss the role of Rebecca as a guardian angel. How does her approach to helping Chloe change throughout the story?

- What lessons does Chloe learn about the true meaning of success and happiness?
- How does the author use secondary characters (like Mr. Jenkins or Maggie) to enhance the story?
- Discuss the theme of forgiveness in the novel. How do different characters demonstrate or struggle with forgiveness?
- How does the book explore the concept of "home"? What does Chloe discover about where she belongs?
- What role does the past play in shaping the characters' present actions and attitudes?
- How does the author use the various Christmas events (like the pageant or the market) to reveal character and advance the plot?
- Discuss the epilogue from Rebecca's perspective. How does it tie together the themes of the book?
- How does this book challenge or reinforce your own ideas about the "Christmas spirit" or the importance of community?
- How does the author use the contrast between Chloe's initial cynicism and the town's enthusiasm for Christmas to drive the narrative?
- Discuss the significance of Chloe's grandmother's house. How does it serve as a bridge between her past and present?

- How does the toy drive subplot contribute to both Chloe's character development and her relationship with Oliver?
- Examine the role of technology and modernization in the story, particularly in relation to Hanks' Department Store. What does this say about balancing tradition and progress?
- How does the author use food and shared meals to develop relationships and advance the plot?

Also by Erica Penrod

Billionaire Bachelor Cove Series

Cowboy Reality Romance Series

Heaven and A Cowboy Series

My Heart Channel Romance Series

Country Brides Cowboy Boots Series

Mountain Cove Series

Billionaire Academy Series

The Lone Horse Ranch

Snowed In For Christmas Series

Diamond Cove Romantic Comedy Series

By E.B Penrod

Ever Eden

About the Author

Erica is a romance-loving storyteller, a certified organizer, and Diet Pepsi enthusiast, who has written over 25 contemporary romance novels. Inspired by her family's rodeo lifestyle, her stories often feature galloping horses and wild romance. But that's not all! When she's not penning heart-fluttering tales, Erica transforms into E.B. Penrod, crafting enchanting romantasy novels. Whether you're in the mood for a swoon-worthy love story or something with a supernatural twist, Erica's got you covered.